Tales of
Irish Enchantment

Patricia Lynch

Illustrated by
FRANCES BOLAND

MERCIER PRESS

MERCIER PRESS
PO Box 5, 5 French Church Street, Cork
16 Hume Street, Dublin 2

© Mercier Press, 1980

ISBN 0 85342 790 9

Trade enquiries to CMD DISTRIBUTION,
55a Spruce Avenue, Stillorgan Industrial Park, Blackrock, Dublin

14 13 12 11 10 9 8 7 6 5

Printed in Ireland by Colour Books Ltd.

CONTENTS

1

MIDIR AND ETAIN

1. The Bride of the High King

HE High King of Ireland, Eochy, had sent a proclamation to all the chiefs and nobles to come to the assembly at Tara.

In a few days messengers began to arrive from every fort and dun. To Eochy's anger not one would come.

'We will not bring our wives and daughters to Tara where there is no Queen to receive them!' came every answer.

Eochy knew they were right, so he sent another proclamation throughout Ireland. He would choose among the noble and beautiful maidens willing to share his throne. He heard of many but the one he thought most of was Etain, daughter of Etar, and at once he rode out to visit her.

On his way to Etar's dun, Eochy came to a spring where a group of girls had gathered. He checked his horse and from the hilltop looked down on them.

One sat in the middle, combing her hair with a comb of gold and silver. She wore a tunic of green silk and over her shoulders was flung a purple mantle. Her golden hair fell in two long plaits, with golden balls at the end.

Eochy's eyes were keen and he could see her vivid blue eyes, with thin black eyebrows, and he heard her clear laughter. He had never seen anyone so lovely.

'She must have come from a fairy palace!' he thought. 'If she is willing I'll make her Queen of all Ireland!'

When Etain met the King and saw how much he loved her, she was indeed willing. So she became his wife and

5

Eochy brought her to Tara.

Etain was happy in her new home until there came to the Court a wonderful musician and storyteller. No one knew where he came from and no one before had heard the music he played, the songs he sang and the stories he told. They were all about the Land of Youth and, when Etain fell asleep, she dreamed she was there, while the music he had played still sounded in her ears.

One day when they were alone he told her a story.

'Long ago when the people of Dana were driven from Ireland by the Children of Miled, they disappeared into the Land of Youth. Midir the Proud, Son of Dagda, was married to a girl so beautiful there had never been another to equal her and they called her The Fair. Another princess, Fuamnach, became jealous and, by her spells, changed The Fair into a butterfly. When she saw the quivering, pale, yellow wings and knew the loveliness of the girl still lived in the butterfly Fuamnach raised a violent wind that blew the butterfly out of the palace of Bri Leith.

For seven years The Fair was tossed and driven from one end of Ireland to the other. Her wings were torn and bruised, and she was almost tired of living when one lucky gust hurled her through an archway of Angus's fairy palace on the Boyne. The quivering butterfly hovered, then dropped on a silken cushion, her pale wings drooping.

Angus, who had been watching, stepped near. The Immortals cannot be hidden from one another and he knew the butterfly was an enchanted girl.

"You shall have peace here,' he told her. 'One day we'll find out if there is any way of giving you back your proper form."

Angus had a sunny bower made, sheltered by flowering bushes and walled with roses. Here The Fair lived, seldom venturing from the palace. Her wings healed and grew larger. After the hardships of those seven years she felt content. Yet she wasn't happy.

Fuamnach heard no more of The Fair and was sure she had driven her away, so that she could never return. Then

6

a stranger spoke of a wonderful butterfly, so rare and lovely, Angus had built a special bower to keep it safe.

"A yellow butterfly with black spots!" thought Fuamnach. 'That is The Fair. I will send her wandering again!"

As the yellow butterfly, at the end of a long sunny day, flew to the bower, a bitter wind swept along the river, caught her up and, tossing her into the air, whirled her over and over.

The Fair flew her swiftest, trying to outdistance the tempest, but she could not. Folding her wings, she let herself be carried along. To her amazement, she saw another palace rising before her. For a moment the wind was held back and she darted into a lofty room, quiet and cool.

Had she found her way back to the Dun of Angus? wondered The Fair.

Then she saw the man sitting at a long table, eating a ripe apple. Beside him, sat a woman, looking thoughtfully into the drinking cup set before her. As she raised it to her lips the wind rose and the yellow butterfly was flung into the wine. Before she could stop herself, the woman drank the wine, butterfly and all.

By her magic powers, Fuamnach heard the news.

"At last I am rid of The Fair!" she thought.

But not long after Etar's wife, the woman who had been drinking the wine when the yellow butterfly was blown into the chieftain's palace, had a baby—a little girl with The Fair's eyes and hair. As she grew she had the enchanted girl's ways and loveliness. She was called Etain and grew up without knowing her real origin, though sometimes she had strange dreams and when she awoke, she felt sad and lost.'

2. Midir Explains

'But my name is Etain!' exclaimed the High King's young wife. 'I am the daughter of Etar and you have told me a story about myself!'

'It is a true story!' declared the musician. 'And I am Midir!'

Etain frowned.

'The story is ended!' she told him.

Midir plucked the strings of his harp and played. Etain listened with eyes half-closed. Now he sang —

> *Etain! In your dreams remember,*
> *Though your waking hours forget.*
> *Here the lonely years have caught you,*
> *Tangled in a magic net.*
>
> *Strange this land of toil and longing;*
> *Sorrow here is wisdom's truth;*
> *Grey the years and grim the visions;*
> *Golden is the Land of Youth.*
>
> *Every day is filled with music;*
> *Every night each moment sings.*
> *Years may pass but time is endless,*
> *Joy's a bird with gleaming wings.*
>
> *Rise up, Etain! I have sought you*
> *Throughout Erin far and near.*
> *Lay your hand in mine and follow.*
> *Etain! You're a stranger here!*
>
> *Where the sunset flames the ocean,*
> *Where the moonbeams cross the sea,*
> *Lies the Land of Youth before us.*
> *Fly there, Etain! Fly with me!*

Etain was dreaming. The magic of the music carried her into the story Midir had told. She smiled, longing to believe him, yet determined not to.

He drew back from the harp and stood up.

'Etain! Will you come with me to the Land of Youth?' She shook her head.

'I am wife to the High King of Ireland. Your stories and your songs are delightful. But don't expect me to believe them!'

Midir looked at her sorrowfully. Then he was gone! The strings of the harp quivered as if he had touched them in passing.

3. A Game of Chess

When the High King returned Etain told him all that had happened. When she repeated Midir's story it became real. She believed it. She sang for the High King the words Midir had sung for her. Then tears came into her eyes and she could not go on.

'It's as well this musician has departed!' declared King Eochy. 'You were wise not to give too much heed to him, Etain.'

That night and many nights following, Etain dreamed she was lost and searching for the way home. When she awoke and found herself in the royal palace at Tara she still felt lost.

Early one summer day, before the gates were open and while Etain still slept, Eochy walked upon the rampart, looking over the wide plain of Breg.

Without sound or motion a young warrior stood beside him. The stranger wore a purple tunic and his yellow hair reached his shoulders. In one hand he carried a light spear. On his arm was a shield with gems set all round it. His eyes, as he gazed upon the High King, were grey and sparkling, and Eochy was puzzled, for he knew this man had not been in Tara the night before and he could not have entered that morning.

'I have come to ask your protection,' said the stranger and he saluted the High King.

'I give welcome to the hero who is yet unknown,' replied Eochy. 'Come with me.'

They entered the great hall and went up to the high table.

'I long to play a game of chess with the best player in all

Ireland,' the young man told the king.

Eochy loved chess even more than music and singing. He sent for his board of silver marked with precious stones and the carved men in the bag of golden chains, so that they could begin at once.

'What stakes shall we play for?' asked the High King, who knew that few could beat him.

'If I lose I will give you fifty dark grey steeds, eager, spirited, yet so trained they will stop at a touch — or a gift of equal worth,' promised the strange warrior.

Eochy considered this.

'I'd rather have something that will be useful to my people,' he decided. 'If I win, let rocks and stones be cleared from the plain of Breg, dig out the rushes that make the land barren, build a causeway across yonder bog and cut down that corner of the forest. Do you agree?'

'You shall have that and more—if you win!' promised the stranger.

And he let Eochy win.

The High King knew his opponent was no mortal and he was thankful to have gained so much. But he was cautious.

'What can this stranger really want with me?' he wondered, as they followed the steward to make sure the task was well done.

A host of fairy folk were already at work. Eochy noticed how they harnessed the oxen, with a yoke upon their shoulders instead of a strap over their foreheads. Afterwards he always had it done this way.

Then the High King and the stranger returned to their game. This time the winner was to choose the forfeit.

Now the stranger won.

'I choose a kiss from Etain!' he said.

Eochy sprang to his feet, knocking over the board and the chessmen.

'Who are you?' he demanded.

'I am Midir!' answered the handsome stranger.

'The musician?'

'Midir the Proud, son of the Dagda, Prince of Slieve

Callary. Etain was my wife over a thousand years ago. She was exiled from our Land of Youth by a cruel spell and all these years I have searched for her. By chance, coming to your Court as a musician, I found her. She will not come with me, so let me have the one kiss!'

Eochy listened without speaking. He loved Etain dearly and he was afraid.

'Return in a month's time!' he said at last. 'Then if Etain is willing, you shall have what you ask.'

4. Midir's Return

The High King had many worried hours dreading what would happen when Midir came to redeem the promise he had made. He told Etain of the games of chess and she was troubled too. Sometimes the king's Court seemed far away and she entered a country of dreamlike loveliness. As the day for Midir's arrival drew near, she began to dread his coming.

'Yet he can do nothing unless I agree,' she told herself.

Before the day came Eochy had the great hall of Tara surrounded by armed men. As darkness fell and the scullions ran along the walls, lighting the torches, a golden radiance dimmed the glow from the fire and the first flickerings of the torches — and Midir stood before the High King.

Etain, who was pouring wine, let the cup fall and stared at him. She heard music, though the harp stood silent, and voices called her — 'Etain! Etain!'

Midir took her hand in his and, throwing his arm about her, they rose into the air. The roof opened and, for a moment, Eochy saw them hovering.

He rushed from the hall but all he or the shouting crowd could see was two swans flying towards Slievenamon.

Etain was never again seen at the Court of the High King.

2

THE THREE SORROWS OF STORYTELLING

THE QUEST OF THE SONS OF TURENN

UGH was a magic craftsman in the days of Nuada of the Silver Hand and in the struggle against the Fomorians he led the Danaans while his father Kian went north to bring the fighting men of Ulster down to join in the war.

As Kian journeyed over the Plain of Murthemney, near Dundalk, he saw three young men, Brian, Iuchar and Iucharba, sons of Turenn.

For years there had been a feud between the two families and Kian, knowing how important it was for him not to delay, determined to avoid his enemies. But they had seen him, knew who he was and called him to come back. Kian could not fight the three and was wondering how he could escape when he saw a herd of pigs trotting across the plain. At once he turned himself into a pig and joined the herd. Though he rooted in the earth and went upon four legs, Brian knew him. Throwing his spear he wounded Kian and the other pigs fled grunting, leaving him lying alone upon the grass.

'Let me become a man again,' he begged as the brothers came up to him.

'I'd always sooner kill a man than a pig!' declared Brian.

And there stood Kian, blood pouring from his wound and his legs trembling with weakness.

'You may kill me!' he said. 'But I have beaten you. If you slayed a pig you would have to pay only the fine of a

14

pig. But now you will slay a man and the world has never heard of a greater fine than the one you shall pay. And though there are no witnesses, the weapons you use shall cry the truth to my avenger.'

'Lay down your swords and spears,' Brian ordered his brothers. 'There must be no weapons to betray us.'

Then they stoned Kian until he died.

The moment this terrible deed was done Iuchar and Iucharba felt remorseful.

'I wish Kian stood alive before us!' said Iuchar.

But Brian had no regrets.

'He was our enemy, the enemy of our father, Turenn, and of all our house. I would kill him seven times over. Bury him now and make an end of it.'

They piled stones over Kian's body, but the stones fell away and would not hide it.

They gathered earth and grass, and built a great mound but the earth slipped down and Kian's body lay exposed once more.

Six times they tried and at last they dug a pit, laid the body there and piled earth and stones until it was level, then stamped the grass down on top so that no one could tell what had happened.

When Kian did not return, Lugh went in search of him. As the drew near the pit the stones over his father's body cried out —

'Here lies Kian, stoned to death by the Sons of Turenn. Avenge him! Avenge him!'

'I will avenge you, my father!' promised Lugh.

He set off for Tara and, before the High King, surrounded by his Court, Lugh denounced the Sons of Turenn.

They could not deny what they had done and Lugh was given the choice of having them killed for their crime, or to name what fine he would accept.

'I choose the fine,' said Lugh. 'If it is too great you must decide.'

'Let us hear it from you,' said the High King.

'Here is the fine!' declared Lugh. 'Three apples, the skin

of a pig, a spear, a chariot with two horses, seven swine, a hound, a cooking spit and three shouts on a hill. That is the fine I am asking!'

'That is a strange fine,' said the High King thoughtfully, 'a very strange fine!'

'Is it too great?' demanded Lugh.

'Indeed it is not!' cread Brian. 'A hundred times as much would not be too great!'

The brothers gripped one another's hands. They had expected death. They knew they deserved it. They could not believe their good fortune. Now, even Brian, they repented the evil they had done.

Lugh spoke again.

'Perhaps it would be well for me to explain the fine?'

'It would be well indeed,' agreed the High King.

Brian was startled. As they listened, he and his brothers wondered if death might not have been an easier fine.

For the three apples were the golden ones that grow in the garden of the sun. The skin belonged to Tuis, King of Greece. It healed all wounds and sickness and would turn water into wine.

'And the spear?' asked Brian, thinking gloomily of the spear which had wounded Kian.

'The spear is called the Luin,' Lugh told him. 'It is owned by the King of Persia and its fiery head is kept in a jar of water so that it will not burn down the palace.

'Then the horses and chariot — you will find them with Dobar, King of Siogair. Sea and land are the same to them and I know of no faster horses.

'The seven pigs are in the herd of Asal, King of the Golden Pillars. If killed and eaten at night, they will be found whole and alive next day. The hound is Fail-Inis, belonging to the King of Ioruiadh, the cold country. All the wild beasts of the world fear Fail-Inis. It will be hard to get her.

'The cooking spit is the spit of the women of Finchory, the sunken island.'

'And the three shouts?' asked Brian.

16

'The three shouts must be given on the hill of Mochaen, in the north of Lochlann. Mochaen and his sons are under *geis* not to allow any shouts to be given on that hill. It was with them my father got his learning,' said Lugh. 'And if I forgave you his death, they would not. That is the fine I ask of you — slayers of Kian!'

The sons of Turenn stood silent and there wasn't a word from King or Court as they went out despairingly to seek their father and tell him their fate.

Turenn tried not to show his dismay.

'Go to Manannan,' he said, 'and ask for the loan of Aonbarr, his horse. If he refuses, ask for the loan of his curragh, Sweeper of the Waves. He will give that, for he is under bond not to refuse a second request and the boat will be the better for you.'

And that was the way it happened.

Their sister Ethne went with them to Brugh na Boyna, where the boat lay.

'How sad it is to see you driven from your own country,' she said. 'But it was a terrible deed to kill Kian and, whatever harm comes to you, it will be just.'

'Don't say that, Ethne,' pleaded Brian. Fierce to the whole world he loved Ethne even more than he loved his brothers. 'We are in good spirits and will do our best to succeed. We would rather be killed a hundred times than die as cowards.'

'I know that,' replied Ethne sadly as they pushed off and, whispering to the magic boat Sweeper, told it where they wanted to go.

At last they came to the Garden of the Sun, in the East of the World.

Dark, proud Brian had always been their leader and, though he had brought such trouble on them, his brothers still obeyed him. He changed himself and them into swift hawks. They flew over the high walls of the garden. All around them were armed men, watching for thieves. They flung their spears at the hawks, but Brian darted high into the air and his brothers after him. They did not go too far, but hovered until the men had cast all their spears. Then the three birds swooped upon the trees, each seizing a golden apple, and sped away.

The King of the Garden had three wise daughters. They heard the guards shouting and, running to the windows of the palace, saw three hawks each carrying a golden apple in its claws, fly towards the shore. At once they turned themselves into ospreys and, chasing the hawks, sent flashes of lightning about them, scorching their wings.

Brian made himself with Iuchar and Iucharba into swans. They dived under the waves and, when they came to the surface, the ospreys had turned home and their magic boat lay peacefully upon the water.

'Now we must journey to Greece,' said Brian. 'If we appear as poets they'll let us in without any trouble. But we need a poem.'

The Sons of Turenn had been well taught, though they were better at fighting than at making poetry. But, between them, they managed a short one all about the skin of a pig.

The Sweeper brought the brothers straight to the harbour steps. But as they stepped ashore, a guard stopped them.

'We have come with a poem to King Tuis!' declared Brian proudly. And they were allowed to pass.

The Court was crowded with poets who hoped to be rewarded. The strangers were asked to recite first and Brian spoke his piece about the pig skin.

'That's a good poem!' declared the King. 'But I'd like it better if it weren't all about my pig skin. What reward do you ask, stranger poet?'

'The pig skin itself, your majesty,' replied Brian, bowing low.

'I couldn't give you that,' said the King of Greece. 'It's the most valuable possession I have. But I'll give you the fill of it in gold three times, though you have given me only one poem.'

The brothers went with the servants to measure the gold. They saw the skin hanging on the wall above the treasure chest. Suddenly, drawing his sword, Brian snatched the skin

18

and raced through the palace, Iuchar and Iucharba close behind and the three of them fought their way through guards and poets until they came to the king upon his throne.

'Was my poem not worth the skin of a pig?' cried Brian in anger, striking him down, then rushing on.

They were badly wounded but as they drew the skin over them lying in the boat Sweeper their wounds soon healed.

'We must be poets once more,' said Brian, as they drew near the Persian coast. 'This time the poem must be worthy of our clan and our quest.'

'But we're warriors, not poets!' protested Iuchar.

'Then let our fighting be better than ever. But a poem of some kind we must have!'

Brian sang the Song of the Spear at the Court of the King of Persia —

Weapon of Heroes,
Swift, bright, sharp;
Slender and fine
As the strings of a harp.

Weapon of heroes,
Sure, arrow-swift,
Victor in battle
Where death is the gift.

Spear of the rain:
Spear of the sun:
Light into darkness:
Journey begun.

Warriors dauntless
Grip shield and spear.
Yonder the foemen,
Charge without fear.

Weapon of heroes,
Strong hand, sure eye.
We, Sons of Turenn,
Conquer or die!

His voice rose so clear and sweet that all who heard shouted their praise and his brothers felt sure the fiery spear would be given to Brian.

But the king refused. Then Brian flung a golden apple knocking him from his throne and the brothers fought from room to room until they discovered the fiery spear, Luin, head downwards in a jar of water.

Whirling it about his head, Brian, his brothers on each side, forced their way through the palace to the courtyard and back to their boat.

'Soon we shall return,' said Iuchar hopefully. 'After these great deeds our crime will pass from men's minds and we shall be greeted as heroes.'

'Lugh will never forget or forgive,' sighed Brian. 'And our hardest trials are before us.'

Leaving the apples, the skin and the spear safely hidden in their boat, they went on shore at Siogair and took service as soldiers with King Dobar.

At the end of a week they brought the golden apples, the pig skin and the fiery spear to their lodgings in case they might be able to use them in gaining the marvellous horses.

A month went by and though they heard people talk of the chariot and the steeds, they had not seen them or been allowed near their stable.

They went to the king and Brian complained that he did not trust them, so they could not stay.

'When we are asked we must always answer we have not set eyes on the king's horses!' declared Brian.

The Sons of Turenn were the best soldiers Dobar had known and he dreaded losing them. So he sent for the chariot and horses.

'Land and water are the same to them,' he boasted. 'If

you searched the world you would not find a more beautiful chariot. It is inlaid with jewels. Those tiny paintings are perfect and the parts are so fitted no human eye can see the joins.'

As he boasted the horses galloped by. Brian gave a sudden leap, flung out the driver, dragged his brothers after him and, handing the fiery spear to Iuchar to beat off attackers, drove to where the Sweeper was hidden.

By this time the story of their quest was being told throughout the countries of the world and, when they journeyed to the land of the King of the Golden Pillars to capture the seven immortal swine, a great friendly host swarmed along the shore.

King Asal dismounted from his horse to welcome them.

'Is it true that you've taken golden apples from the Garden of the Sun, the magic pig skin from the King of Greece, the fiery spear and Dobar's horses and chariot, and that all the guards and soldiers in the world can't hold you back?' he asked.

'It is indeed true!' said Brian.

'Why have you done this?' asked Asal.

Brian told him the whole story.

'And now you've come to take my seven pigs?'

'I must have them!' declared Brian.

King Asal stood thinking, his arms folded. The brothers watched him sadly. They did not want to kill or rob this pleasant man. But they needed the pigs.

At last Asal laughed.

'Take the pigs as a gift,' he said. 'We can managed without them and I won't bring my people into a fight. Rest and feast here for a day and the pigs will be ready for you.'

This was the first day the Sons of Turenn had been happy since they killed Kian.

'Where are you going from here?' the King asked them.

'To Ioruaidh, the cold country. The king has a hound called Fail-Inis and that hound is part of our fine.'

'My daughter is his wife. I'll come with you and ask him to give up the hound without a struggle,' declared King Asal.

But the king of Ioruaidh would not give his hound. He brought out his soldiers and attacked the invaders. In the fight Brian was separated from Iuchar and Iucharba, but he defeated the king and handed him over to his father-in-law. Asal gave them the hound and they said goodbye.

'I am tired of fighting and wandering!' exclaimed Iucharba. 'We'll be old men before our quest is finished.'

'It is finished now!' Brian told him.

The younger man stared at him, then nodded, for Lugh had put the spell of forgetfulness upon them and they thought their quest was indeed ended.

Gladly they turned the Sweeper homewards and, coming unexpectedly to the Court at Tara, found Lugh there and gave him the prizes.

'Where is the cooking spit?' he asked. 'And have you given three shouts on a hill?'

They did not answer, but went away in silence. Holding hands as they used to when they were children they walked slowly to their father's fort.

They told Turenn and their sister Ethne of their fights and wanderings, and of how Lugh had treated them.

'It is my enmity with Kian which has brought all these disasters upon you,' grieved Turenn.

And Ethne wept because she could not help her brothers.

For weeks and months they searched for the island of Finchory. Then a passing fisherman told them it was under the waves. Brian put on his water dress and leapt into the sea. Down, down he went until he landed among rocks and seaweed. He followed a path of crushed shells and came at last to the island of Caer of the Fair Hair — Finchory.

Brian saw a great hall built of coral with fishes swimming in and out of long, high openings. He entered by the largest and found a hundred and fifty women feasting, singing, doing embroidery. They watched as Brian strode among them and seized the spit from the hearth. Then they burst into laughter and the fair woman who sat on a throne of iridescent shells, decorated with green seaweed, told him that even if his brothers had come too, the smallest girl there could have stopped the three of them.

'But as you are so brave, Brian, take the spit and welcome,' she added.

He was very weary when his brothers saw him swimming at a distance, turned the boat after him, and pulled him on board.

'We had almost given you up,' said Iuchar.

'There is but one task left now,' said Brian.

They journeyed to the Hill of Mochaen. They came quietly in the darkness. But Mochaen and his sons, fully armed, were watching. Swords uplifted they rushed together and fought through the night. As the sun rose, the brothers put their spears through the guardians of the hill. But the Sons of Turenn were so wounded they could scarcely stand. Brian lifted his brothers and held them up with his arms around them as they gave three feeble shouts.

'The *Eric* (fine) is paid!' whispered Brian as they stumbled to their boat.

By the time they reached home they were very near death. Ethne watched over them while Turenn himself went with the spit to Lugh.

'My sons have paid their fine,' he said. 'But they are worn with danger and hardship, and life is going from them. Lend the magic skin to save them.'

'I would not save them for all the gold in the world,' replied Lugh. 'You shall not have the skin!'

Turenn went back. Brian lay between Iuchar and Iucharba, and their life went.

'Each had the making of a King of Ireland!' said Turenn sadly. 'Brian, the leader; Iuchar, the comrade, and Iucharba, the good, silent follower.'

Then he lay down beside them and died too.

3

THE THREE SORROWS OF STORYTELLING

THE SWAN CHILDREN

LIR was one of the five Danaan Kings who ruled in Ireland before the coming of the Milesians. His fort was at The Hill of The White Field on Slieve Fuad in Armagh, just beyond the Gap of the North. Bov, the Red (Bov Ruadh) was another Danaan King and Lir married one of his foster daughters, Eva. They had twin children, Fionuala and Hugh. A few years later Fiacha and Conn were born and Eva died, for not all the Danaans were immortal.

Lir loved his children, but he loved Fionuala more than the three boys put together. Only for her he would have died when he lost Eva. Still he was lonely and every corner of the Fort reminded him of his sorrow. At last he took the children with him to stay at the Palace of Bov Ruadh.

Bov had a big family and all his relations lived with him. They tried to make Lir happy again and Aoife, another of Bov's foster daughters, was so beautiful and kind, that Lir could not let a day pass without driving with her.

She made him forget his loneliness. His mind become so filled with Aoife there was no room for Eva's memory. One day she asked him when he would be going home. Then he understood what had happened. He could not return without her, for he loved Aoife as once he had loved Eva.

Aoife was willing to marry him, to leave the gay, crowded palace of Bov and go to Lir's solitary Fort; willing to be a mother to his children.

25

It seemed to Fionuala no time at all when they were travelling home with a new mother — a step-mother!

Aoife was good to the children and they were fond of her, though Fionuala never forgot her real mother. She was a wise, lovely child and Lir hated to leave her behind when he was forced to travel to distant parts of his kingdom.

While Lir was away Aoife ruled the Fort. She was clever and made herself so agreeable that her orders were obeyed without any trouble at all. Lir was delighted with this new life and thankful that Aoife cared for the children as if she were their own mother.

Each time he left home he came back with his chariot piled with presents. Aoife's were the grandest he could find — a necklace of square-cut purple stones set in dull silver: a silk frock the colour of moonbeams, so fine she could draw it through her closed hand without crushing: a pair of golden slippers sown with tiny pearls.

Aoife smiled at the little spears and shields Lir brought the boys. Though exquisitely made they were only toys. But when she saw Fionuala's tiny chariot with paintings on the sides, so beautiful everyone cried out in delight, her eyes darkened.

'Lir must have searched the country to find such perfection.' she thought. 'He loves his daughter as much as he loves me!'

From that day Aoife changed, but only Fionuala noticed.

She hid her presents, but Aoife grew more and more jealous, even of the boys.

Fionuala asked her father to bring her the same kind of presents as he brought her brothers, but now it was impossible to satisfy Aoife.

She tried to conceal her hatred, but Fionuala understood.

'I cannot go on living with them!' thought Aoife, and she determined to be rid of her step-children while their father was away.

On a fine spring morning Aoife told Fionuala she would take her and her brothers to visit their grandfather, Bov the Red. The boys were delighted, for there they would meet other boys. But Fionuala, without knowing why, was afraid.

She stood watching the men harnessing the horses to the chariot when the charioteer stepped over to her.

'Do not come on this journey, Fionuala!' he whispered. 'Hide yourself so that you cannot be found until we have departed.'

Ready to obey him, for he had served her mother for years, the girl ran to look for her brothers. They came running towards her, but following slowly was Aoife and Fionuala knew she was too late.

'Couldn't we wait until my father returns?' she asked. 'Suppose he comes while we are away?'

'I will be here seven days before him,' replied Aoife. 'You need not trouble about him.'

Fionuala was more frightened than before, but she had to climb into the chariot.

The morning mist still lay on the fields as the horses galloped off. The boys were so excited they did not notice how still and quiet their sister sat beside them, or the gloomy face of the charioteer.

At each rise or bend of the road Fionuala looked back as though she knew she would never see her home again.

They were growing tired when Aoife stopped the chariot at Crooked Wood beside Lake Derryvaragh.

'Do as I warned you!' she ordered the charioteer. 'Kill these children.'

'This is an evil deed, Aoife!' he answered. 'I cannot do it!'

Taking his spear from the chariot he broke the haft and flung away the pieces.

'Run!' he said to Fionuala. 'You will not be followed.'

He knew that the white horses would obey no one but himself, not even Aoife, and the children were fast runners. But they clung to one another and gazed despairingly about them.

Where could they run? Fionuala stared at the lake. Could they hide among the rushes?

Pulling Conn, the smallest boy, by the hand she ran

27

towards the water. The other boys reached the shore first. But as they paused, at the water's edge, Aoife lifted her light throwing spear. Yet, though she hated the four, she could not kill them one by one. Letting the spear fall she stretched out her magic rod and laid this spell upon them.

'Live, but not as children. From this moment you shall be creatures of air and water. The land shall no longer know you. Children of Lir — be as swans!'

Fionuala felt her neck growing long. Her golden hair, her clothes changed to feathers. Her arms became wings and looking at her brothers she saw them changing into snow white swans.

'Why have you done this?' Fionuala asked her step-mother. 'What harm have we done? How can you be so cruel?'

'This is the doom I lay upon you!' chanted Aoife.

'Three hundred years upon the lake of Derryvaragh.

Three hundred upon the stormy Straits of Moyle.

Three hundred where the Western Ocean rolls in by Inish Glory.'

'When will this terrible enchantment end?' asked Fionuala.

Aoife looked at her little step-daughter and a touch of pity came into her heart.

'When the Woman of the South shall wed the Man from the North and a thin cold bell rings through the land, then Nuala, the hour of your release is near,' she answered, and stepped into the chariot.

As the driver, with a sorrowful glance at the swans, leaped beside her and gathered up the reins, Aoife looked over her shoulder —

'This I leave you — your power of speech and the gift of song.'

Away dashed the white horses carrying Aoife out of sight.

The four swan children huddled together.

'Our father will soon find us,' said Fionuala, 'or perhaps we'll wake up and find that we have wronged Aoife and this

28

is only a dream.'

On went the chariot, the driver urging the horses, for he hoped that Bov Ruadh would be able to lift the spell. No doubt he would send a messenger to Lir and surely that learned king would yet save the children. Aoife sat proudly, one moment delighted at her deed, the next wondering what would happen when it was discovered.

Bov stood upon the terrace of his palace but, when he saw Aoife without the children, he hurried to meet her.

Before he could speak the charioteer flung down the reins and sprang to the ground.

'Aoife has enchanted the children!' he cried. 'They are now swimming upon Derryvaragh Lake — four snow white swans.'

Bov the Red looked at the Queen in amazement.

'Can this be true?' he asked.

Aoife gazed back without a trace of fear.

'It is true!' she declared. 'Lir loved his children more than me. My jealousy has grown so great I could not bear it and they are his no longer. You cannot take off the spell. My magic is more powerful than yours.'

Bov struggled to speak.

'I can't help them, the poor unfortunate children. But I can punish you! If Lir's home is theirs no longer, it is also lost to you.' He lifted his rod. 'Go forth into the wilderness of space and darkness, foul demon of the air!'

With a scream, Aoife changed from a beautiful woman into a thin shivering waif and was swept away up into the air. She was never heard of again.

Bov the Red sent his swiftest horse and rider in search of Lir, who came at once. As the sun rose the two kings journeyed to Lake Derryvaragh. There they found the four swan children weeping but still unable to believe that they must live as birds for nine hundred years.

When they saw Lir, they swam close in to the shore. He put his arms about the boys and stroked Nuala's white feathers as once he had caressed her long gleaming hair. She could talk to him and she and her brothers were sure their troubles were over now their father had found them.

But for all his power Lir could not remove the spell Aoife had put upon his children. They could speak as human beings and, like all the Danaans, they were clever musicians and singers. Now they sang so wonderfully that from all the distant parts of Ireland people came to hear them.

Slowly they became used to their strange life and, while the Swan Children stayed on Lake Derryvaragh, great peace and kindliness spread throughout the country. There were no quarrels; fighting ceased and each day seemed happier than the last.

Lir camped beside the lake and for him and the children those three hundred years passed like three days.

Bov the Red sent a proclamation throughout the land that, for the sake of the Swan Children, no swan should ever again be killed in Ireland.

The time came when Fionuala and her brothers had to say goodbye to their own people, rise up from Derryvaragh and fly to the wild desolate northern coast, to the Straits of Moyle between Ireland and Alba.

They came to Moyle in winter. Day after day a bitter wind sent the waves dashing against Seals Rock, the most sheltered spot they could find. The spray was frozen and the air so thick with snow they could scarcely see one another. Fionuala drew her brothers under her wings, sheltering them from the worst cold. She told them the stories she had heard in their father's home. She taught them all she knew, so that their minds had thoughts beyond their present unhappiness. She sang the songs learned before Aoife put the spell upon them and travellers, hearing her sad lovely voice far off, wondered if it came from sea or air.

Wild the wind and cold the night;
Sing and dream till morning's light.

Grey the sky and fierce the sea;
Bitter is our misery.

Sorrow makes the hours long.
Suffering should follow wrong.

We have done no evil deed.
Lonely is the life we lead.

Sad the hours and days and years;
Salt the waves and salt my tears.

Shall I ever hear that bell
Cruel Aoife did foretell?

Cold and sweet and silver clear,
Filled with comfort, yet with fear.

Sad my dream and sad my song.
Hours, days and years are long.

'If we went on shore,' said Conn, 'we could find shelter.'
Fionuala shook her head.

'We cannot go on shore until our doom is coming to an
end.'

'Then we won't always be like this?' he asked eagerly.

'Not always!'

Even summer was harsh in this wild region. They were
lonely, for their people could not come to them and there
were no dwellings along that rocky coast. Fishing boats
from the islands of Alba kept to the north and only wandering birds ventured near. They sang of strange lands where
the sun was hot and great forests spread over plains and
climbed mountains, where rivers were mighty as the sea.

'There are amazing birds in those far countries,' the birds
told the swans. 'Some glow like jewels, others dwell on
mountain tops and fly so high they are lost in the clouds.
We have heard birds singing so that we longed to stay and
listen for ever. But never have we heard such singing as
yours.'

Sea birds nested in the cliffs and the Swan Children

watched them building homes, bringing up their young ones, swimming, fishing, quarrelling. But they were not friendly. They pretended not to see these swans who spoke like human beings and sang so sadly.

The Children of Lir found happiness in swimming and flying, in their affection for one another and in talking of what would become of them when their time of enchantment was over. Even that three hundred years came to an end, yet they were no older than when they had driven with Aoife to Lake Derryvaragh. Sometimes they thought they had been swans only a short while and once Hugh dreamed his father came to take him home. But he woke as he was stepping into the chariot.

Next day the worst storm they had known raged along the Straits of Moyle. The waves rose against the cliffs and the swans were separated. Fionuala saw her brothers beaten under the sea. She called them but the screaming wind prevented them hearing her voice as she was swept away.

'If only I find them, I'll never grumble again whatever happens,' she thought.

At dawn, bruised and weary, their wings tattered, the four swans found one another. First to Seals Rock came Fionuala, then Hugh, flying down the wind and a little while after, Conn and Fiachra.

'We are going west,' said Fionuala. 'I think we will never suffer so much again.'

They flew across Ireland by night. When they saw far below the glow of fires and the fluttering light of torches, the Swan Children wondered if ever they would live within walls and know the happiness of being with friends in their own home.

They flew down near Erris Point in north-west Mayo. There, among the bird islands, they entered upon the last three hundred years of their doom.

They felt lonelier than ever and one winter, the sea around the islands from Erris to Aran was frozen so that they could not swim. A young farmer named Evric heard them singing and going out in the early morning, watched until he discovered the enchanted swans. Soon he became their friend and heard their story and each day he came to talk with them.

'It is time we went to look at our father's palace!' Fionuala told her brothers.

Gaily they rose up into the cold grey air and flew over the frozen land, Fionuala leading, Hugh close beside her and the younger brothers a little behind.

'It should be here!' declared Fionuala.

'There is no palace, or halls, or buildings of any kind. Our father's home cannot be here!' said Hugh.

The others joined them and circling round, they tried to discover some trace of King Lir's palace.

All they could see were a few grass-grown mounds, withered bushes and patches of nettles.

'It cannot be here!' cried Fiachra.

'It is here!' Fionuala told him.

Now she realised that their own land was hidden from them. They would never see their people again.

This was the most unhappy day in their whole lives. Mournful and bewildered, they returned to the wild shore where they had made their home and saw Evric wandering along the frozen strand, searching anxiously for them.

'I feared you might never come back!' he said.

'We went to seek the palace of Lir,' Fionuala told him. 'But the doom that is on us has hidden everything we knew.'

Suddenly the thin sound of a bell rang through the air. Startled, the three brothers drew together. But Fionuala remembered.

'It is the bell whose ringing foretells our release,' she said. 'And yet I am afraid!'

'Don't be afraid!' cried the young man. 'There dwells the one who will understand these mysteries. Wait here for me!'

With him came the hermit Mocahovog who had built his cell and a chapel on one of the rocky inlets. His long white robe, his noble face and friendly eyes, comforted Fionuala.

'Here is another friend,' she thought.

'Peace be with you, Children of Lir!' he called.

'Peace!' echoed the swans.

They came close to the shore, while he seated himself on a flat rock, and looked at him in silence.

'Long ago I heard of the singing swans.' said the old man, 'I prayed that one day I might come to know them. Tell me your history.'

'We were four happy children,' began Fionuala.

The old man and the young did not move or speak as the swans recalled the joys of their early days and all the misery that followed. Evric hid his face and wept but the hermit seemed caught in a dream.

Fionuala's head drooped with weariness as she finished.

'Aoife was cruel,' said the hermit gently. 'She drove you from the Land of Youth and closed its gates against you. But God has spared you for a great destiny.'

Then day by day he taught Fionuala and her brothers the Christian faith, of how Ireland had changed with the coming of the Milesians and of St Patrick's teaching. Slowly the long sad years slipped from their minds and they sang for Evric and the old hermit as once they sang for the Danaans, only more enchantingly than ever.

Others heard their singing and crowds gathered on the Mayo shore hoping to catch a glimpse of the swans. But they hid from everyone except their two friends.

The fame of the Children of Lir reached Princess Deoca of Munster who was betrothed to a Connaught chief named Lairgnen. He longed to give Deoca everything she wanted. She asked for only one wedding gift — the four singing swans. Lairgnen, with his warriors, rode to Erris and asked Mocahovog to give up the swans. The hermit refused and though Evric tried to protect them, the Connaught men bound the Children of Lir with golden chains and dragged them off to Deoca.

Evric and the hermit followed all the way to the Court of Munster.

As the swans were brought before the princess their white feathers dropped away. Instead of graceful white birds, or the lovely Danaan children, the horrified Deoca saw four withered creatures incredibly old.

Lairgnen, appalled at what he had done, rushed from the Court, while Evric and the hermit knelt beside Fionuala and her brothers.

'Lay us in one grave,' she said. 'Conn at my right hand and Fiachra at my left. But put Hugh before me, for that was the way I sheltered them in those winter nights upon the Straits of Moyle.'

The hermit baptised them as they died. He and Evric obeyed Fionuala and laid the four in the one grave. So they went to heaven. But the young farmer and the old hermit remembered the Swan Children to the end of their days.

4

THE THREE SORROWS OF STORYTELLING

DEIRDRE AND THE SONS OF USNA

1. The Prophecy

IT was a cold, bitter night with a wind that tore branches from the trees, beat the grass flat and howled about Felim's gay, bright hall. The fires burned clear although the door stood open, for Cathbad, the Druid, was outside, his arms thrust inside his thick robe, his head flung back, gazing at the stars.

Felim wanted to close the door, for King Conor Mac Nessa was his guest that night. The king stood by the fire half-way down the hall, smiling at the leaping flames and listening to Fergus Mac Roy who was complaining that Maeve, the warlike Queen of Connaught, had increased her army by a thousand men.

'That makes her army larger than her husband's, Ailell. He won't be pleased!' said Conor.

'It means their army is already larger than ours!' exclaimed Mac Roy. 'And if King Ailell increases his army to match hers, what's to prevent the pair of them invading Ulster?'

Conor was tired of talk. He was hungry and longed for supper.

'When will the banquet be ready?' he asked impatiently.

'It is ready!' declared Felim. 'If only Cathbad would come in, we could close the doors and the wine would be poured at once. The hot dishes are waiting!'

'I smell them!' said Conor, sniffing with pleasure. 'Pour

the wine. I'll bring the Druid in.'

He strode down the hall and stepped into the starlit night.

Cathbad was motionless. The air was cold and frost glittered on the grass and stone wall surrounding the dun. The king put out his hand to touch the Druid, then drew back. Cathbad's eyes watched the distant horizon and Conor Mac Nessa stared too. A faint sparkle appeared as though a tiny torch had been lit at the edge of the world. On invisible wings it sped across the sky, growing larger and brighter, until it hung for one brief instant about their heads, then rushed on, on, on into the darkness beyond.

Felim came through the doorway.

'The banquet is on the tables. The wine is poured!'

Cathbad sighed and turned towards him.

Before he could speak, a girl came running down the hall, her hair streaming, her face flushed, he eyes wide open with excitement.

'A child for my lord Felim!' she cried; 'a daughter is born! A lovely little girl!'

'We'll drink her health!' said the king, as Felim swung around to go with the girl.

Suddenly Conor changed his mind.

'Wait, Felim! Cathbad has been watching the stars. If he would foretell your little daughter's future, we should all remember this day!'

Cathbad looked once more at the sky, then shook his head.

'We have seen a star born in the darkness, sweep across the sky as if the gods were hunting it, stay over this hall while a man might lift a horn of wine, then dart into the further darkness over the sea.'

He looked sadly at Felim.

'That we have seen. But, in the stars, I read that the child born this night will grow to be the loveliest woman in all Ireland. A king will seek to marry her and, because of this, she will bring death and disaster upon Ulster.'

The warriors belonging to Felim's dun and those who

had come with the king, were listening.

'Kill the child!' cried one.

And the others shouted fiercely—

'Let her die before she can harm Ulster!'

Felim sprang before them, his face white with horror.

'What! Kill a child the night she is born! No man shall harm my daughter!'

Conor Mac Nessa flung his arm about Felim's shoulders.

'Give me the baby,' he said. 'I'll take care of her and when she is grown into her full beauty I'll marry her myself. She shall reign with me as Queen of Ulster. Cathbad's prophecy will be fulfilled, yet be defeated. She shall wed a king, yet bring no harm to Ulster. Now in to the banquet and we'll drink her health.'

Cathbad shook his head slowly.

'Even Conor Mac Nessa cannot cheat fate,' he thought.

2. The Secret Dun

When Connor returned to Emain Macha the baby went with him. He gave her in charge to his old nurse Levarcam and they called the baby Deirdre.

The king had a fort built in the heart of a secret wood and Deirdre lived there with Levarcam and a few servants. As she grew the nurse taught her to embroider her own clothes and the hangings on the walls of her room. Cathbad shared his learning with her, music, the old stores and poems. But, though she coaxed and pleaded, he would not teach her to read the stars.

'If I am a true prophet, sorrow will come upon her soon enough,' he thought. 'Better for her not to know until she must that she is born to disaster.'

Conor came as often as he could leave the Court and he played chess with Deirdre. She practised with Cathbad and Levarcam so that she would surprise him and once succeeded in winning the game.

'You are growing up,' he told her. 'Soon you will indeed

be the loveliest woman in Ireland!'

Conor always arrived alone for he hoped that by keeping Deirdre hidden in that secret place until he married her, the Druid's prophecy would be unfulfilled.

Deirdre was happy though her only young companions were the birds and squirrels. But Levarcam told her of the great Court where she would one day reign and the girl's dreams were always of the wonderful future.

One winter day Deirdre stood upon the rampart of the fort looking at the snow-clad trees. The ground was like a sheet of beaten silver, except that to one side, a splash of blood where a scullion had killed a calf for the dinner, lay in the snow. As Deirdre watched, a raven dropped from a tree and stood there without moving.

'Levarcam,' said Deirdre to the nurse who had come up behind her. 'Last night I dreamed of a young man—not

much older than I am—his hair was the colour of that raven's wing, his cheeks were crimson and his skin was white as snow. In my dream I thought he was the man I would marry.'

'You must not speak that way!' scolded the old woman. 'You know you will marry King Conor!'

'He is so old!' objected Deirdre. 'And I cannot help my dreams.'

'The king is a great man,' Levarcam told her. 'He is kind and has given you everything. At the beginning he even saved your life. When you marry Conor Mac Nessa you will be a queen and there'll be dozens of handsome young men to serve you.'

'Is there a young man at Conor's Court with hair black as a raven's wing, cheeks red as freshly spilled blood and skin white as snow?' asked Deirdre.

Levarcam sighed. Her duty was to the king, but she loved Deirdre.

'There is indeed,' she answered.

'And his name?'

'He is called Naisi!'

'I have seen him!' Deirdre told the nurse.

'How could you?' cried the old woman. 'I have obeyed the king. I have kept you hidden in this wood. You can't have seen Naisi. You are still dreaming.'

'I have seen Naisi!' repeated the girl. 'One day, in the summer, I threw my ball as far as I could and ran after it right to the edge of the trees. As I stood there, looking over the plain, three young men with spears in their hands came towards me. The nearest was Naisi. He was the tallest and his smile was the friendliest. He opened his mouth to speak to me, only I was frightened and ran back here. But I have seen Naisi!'

'Put him out of your mind,' said Levarcam. 'You will marry Conor Mac Nessa.'

'Send a message to Naisi,' pleaded Deirdre. 'You love me! Send a message to bid him come here to me.'

'I dare not!' replied the old nurse.

Deirdre coaxed and pleaded, and, at last, Levarcam gave in.

'I will send the message. The gods grant Naisi will refuse to venture here.'

Deirdre was delighted.

'He will come!' she declared. 'I know Naisi will by the way he looked at me.'

And he came, his brothers Ainle and Ardan with him. They were forced to travel secretly, so it was night when they tapped at the door of the fort. Levarcam opened to them and brought them into the beautifully furnished hall where Deirdre sat on a golden stool, waiting.

Her long green frock was embroidered with gold and her golden hair was entwined with pearls. She was lovelier even than Naisi remembered. He bowed and stared at her in silence. His brothers stood on each side of the doors, swords in their hands.

'I knew you would come, Naisi!' said Deirdre. 'You will save me from the king?'

Naisi looked at her sadly.

'I'd do anything I could for you!' he declared. 'But I cannot act against the king. We three are Red Branch Knights and our oath is to Conor Mac Nessa. And haven't we all heard about the beautiful maiden he plans to marry to save her from the terrible fate foretold by the great Cathbad.'

'Two old men!' exclaimed Deirdre scornfully. 'If you won't help me, I'll go off by myself. Somewhere in Ireland there must be a hero who would protect me!'

She looked so unhappy in her disappointment, so young and lovely, Naisi felt tears rising in his eyes. He turned to his brothers. They had leaned their swords against the door, forgetting they had promised to guard it and their faces were as troubled as Deirdre's.

'You will come with us?' he asked.

'To the edge of the world!' they replied.

Then Deirdre knew she had won and was so happy they all forgot their fear of King Conor and were as delighted as she was.

'We must have a feast in honour of our betrothal!' said Naisi, who was used to the grand ways of the Court.

'Are you enchanted!' exclaimed old Levarcam. 'We must leave this fort at once. Do you not understand that every man and woman in this place is a spy of the king's. Load yourselves with arms and jewels, for all we have now is what can carry.'

3. The Flight

They left the lights burning to make the servants think they were still in the hall. Then silently, on tip-toe, they went out of the fort through the trees. Deirdre did not look back once though this was the only home she had ever known.

First they went to the brothers' own home—the Dun of Usna. There Naisi and Deirdre were married, and his people sheltered them for several days until the news they expected came—that Conor Mac Nessa had discovered Deirdre had fled with Naisi, and was seeking her.

The three men talked together.

'I must go away with Deirdre,' said Naisi. 'To remain here would bring ruin upon us all. What will you do? If you stay Conor's vengeance will fall on you.'

'We will go with you!' replied his brothers.

They told Deirdre.

'I am bringing trouble on those I love,' she sighed. 'The prophecy is coming true.'

'We will leave trouble behind!' said Naisi. 'Four fleet horses and we can laugh at the king!'

They had fleet horses and they were the best riders in all Ireland, so they kept ahead of Conor and his men. But there was neither peace nor rest for them. Where they woke at morning they dared not sleep at night and they all grew weary. Naisi dreaded the day when Deirdre would long for the quiet of the fort in the secret wood.

'We must leave Ireland,' he said to his brothers and sent a message to Levarcam to bring all their goods and meet them with a boat at a certain harbour on the northern sea. There was sadness in Naisi's heart when he told Deirdre they must leave their own country, for life there, with Conor's hatred pursuing them, was impossible.

Deirdre laughed.

'When we are young, that's the time to see the world,' she declared. 'We can always come back!'

'I wonder,' said Naisi.

They sailed to Alba and came at last to Glen Etive by the head of the loch. There they built their home in the shelter of Ben Cruachan. Naisi dreaded the loneliness of Deirdre, but she had never been so happy in her life. While the brothers hunted and explored, she helped Levarcam to make the place pleasant. While the old woman cooked, Deirdre made clothes for all, embroidering them so that they were grandly dressed as if they were still at Emain Macha. They played chess in the evenings, sang, told stories, and Deirdre learned of that land she had left before she knew it. On sunny days they swam and went sailing. Gradually they made friends. Wanderers, boasting of the hospitality given them at the house by Loch Etive, sent curious Scottish chiefs to see the strangers.

There were many feuds and raids in Alba and the Sons of Usna were ready to help their new friends. In time, thought Deirdre, we will forget Conor and all the old trouble.

4. A Message from Conor Mac Nessa

At first King Conor hoped that Deirdre and the Sons of Usna would grow tired of exile and try to return. As the days went by he tried to forget Deirdre, but could not. He remembered those visits to the fort in the secret wood and the charming child who had grown into a girl so lovely she would have been the pride of his Court. He imagined her living a hard rough life, perhaps losing her beauty and becoming weary of Naisi. Then he pitied her.

'If she came back now I would forgive her,' he told himself. 'But not Naisi!'

Then he heard of her happiness and how she and the three brothers had made a new life for themselves in Alba.

His pity turned to anger and he determined on revenge. He could not go to Alba himself. If he sent a messenger asking the exiles to return, they might suspect his motive, unless they trusted the messenger. He considered which of his knights would serve him best and decided on Fergus Mac Roy—his own half-brother.

'Bid them return,' he said. 'I will forgive them and forget the past.'

Fergus Mac Roy had been one of Naisi's dearest friends and had missed him greatly. He was glad to go on such a mission and set off at once. He was welcomed at Loch Etive and they sat up hour after hour listening to the news from home, until dawns showed over the mountains.

'You have not asked what brought me here,' said Fergus, suddenly feeling uneasy.

'You are with us. That is enough,' said Deirdre, smiling at Naisi's friend. But Naisi was startled.

'I thought you came merely in friendship!' he muttered.

'I came because I am your friend!' declared Fergus. 'That is why the king sent me to ask you to return. He forgives and forgets everything.'

'That is not like Conor,' said Naisi wisely.

But the hope of returning to Ireland overcame his mistrust. He turned to Deirdre and saw her frightened face.

'Didn't you hear?' he asked. 'We can go home.'

'This is our home!' cried Deirdre. 'This is where we have have been happy. Don't let us go. I am afraid of Conor. He is a proud, jealous man!'

'Don't you trust Fergus?' declared Naisi. 'He is our protector. While we are with him, no king in Ireland would dare to lay a finger on us!'

Deirdre sat silent. Though she liked and trusted Fergus

she feared Conor Mac Nessa. Her dreams were terrifying and she dreaded their return.

The ship which carried them back to Ireland was the finest any of them had seen. But Deirdre thought longingly of the crowded little boat which had taken them to safety.

'I have lived so many years in simple ways I would feel easier had the boat which carried us away, brought his home,' she murmured.

'Surely you aren't afraid?' asked Naisi. 'I have never known you show such dread.'

'I fear Conor,' replied Deirdre. 'If he forgives, why not leave us in peace?'

'I am older than you,' Naisi told her. 'As you grew older you would become weary in exile. Now there isn't a shadow on my happiness'

Deirdre forced herself to smile and pretended to be excited as they drew near the land.

Baruch, the lord of the Red Branch, was there to greet them.

'I had a feast prepared for the king,' he told Fergus. 'But he sent word that you will take his place while he awaits Deirdre and the Sons of Usna at Emain Macha.'

'I cannot feast with you tonight,' replied Fergus. 'I must first go with Deirdre and Naisi to Emain Macha. Then I will come back to you.'

Baruch frowned.

'You must feast with me tonight!' he protested. 'It is the king's command and I have heard it is a *geis* for you not to refuse a feast.'

Fergus was still unwilling, but he could not refuse.

'This will delay me but the one night,' he said to Naisi. 'My sons, Illan the Fair and Buino the Red, will take charge of you and I'll follow in the morning.'

5. *A Strange Homecoming.*

Lights were shining through the darkness as Deirdre and the Sons of Usna rode up to Emain Macha.

'This is where I should have lived if Naisi had not found me,' thought Deirdre. 'I'm glad I'm not a queen.'

Naisi looked at the great hall looming through the mist, with the red light of fires and the white smoky flare of torches. He showed Deirdre where the king's chambers were and the queen's, wondered at the silence and emptiness, if a banquet had been prepared and why none of the royal guards came to receive them.

A steward of the royal household led them to the Hostel of the Red Branch where fires and beds and a well-laid table waited for them. It was grand, but not so grand as the banqueting hall. Naisi, remembering the music and singing, the shouting and laughter in the old days, was troubled at the silence and loneliness.

Deirdre had never seen so beautiful a house before and she knew nothing of the ways of the Court, nor of the crowds that thronged there.

'Conor must indeed have forgiven us if he lodges us so splendidly,' she said.

Naisi did not answer. He was beginning to fear Conor.

Deirdre, the three brothers and Levarcam, sat together. The old woman was wiser than the four of them and she knew they were in terrible danger.

'If only they'd asked me,' she muttered. 'I'd have told them. I know all about Conor Mac Nessa. Maybe I shouldn't have waited to be asked.'

When they had finished eating and were rested, Levarcam brought out the gold and silver chessmen which she had carried away from the fort in the secret wood, and told the steward to bring a chess board. Deirdre and Naisi always played at least one game before they went to bed at night. Ardan and Ainle sat by the fire talking to Illan and Buino who were polishing their spears.

All this while, Conor sat alone in his big empty banqueting hall, drinking glass after glass of wine and brooding on his vengeance.

Presently he sent a messenger to tell Levarcam he wanted her. The old woman trembled, but she came at once.

'So you are back, Levercam,' he said. 'That was a fine trick you played me.'

Levercam did not answer.

'And the Sons of Usna are back where they belong,' he added.

'They are indeed,' agreed the nurse. 'And the king who has those three lights of valour at his Court need fear no enemy.'

'Deirdre is with them: how is she?' asked Conor quietly, but his eyes glittered.

'She is well,' replied Levercam. 'But her life has been hard and she is no longer the beautiful girl you knew.'

She sighed and the king sighed with her. When she went away he began drinking again.

Still he thought of Deirdre and, at last, told a servant named Trendorn to go to the Red Branch Hostel and find out what the guests were doing.

Trendorn found the door closed and bolted, but looking in at a narrow slit, he could see Deirdre and Naisi playing chess. They were so well matched, the others sat still and silent, watching.

The spy made a noise and Naisi, looking up, caught sight of his face. He seized one of the chessmen and flung it at Trendorn, striking out his eye, then continued the game. With blood streaming from his face Trendorn stumbled back to the king.

'I have seen the loveliest woman in all the world!' he cried. 'But for this unlucky blow I would still be looking at her!'

'So Levarcam cheated me,' thought Conor. 'She cheated me once before. But I think I'll have the better of her this time.'

He called his guards and ordered them to seize Naisi with his two brothers and bring them before him.

The guards marched to the Hostel of the Red Branch. Buino, son of Fergus, met them with his men, and drove them back.

Deirdre and Naisi went on with their game.

'It would be unmannerly for us to defend ourselves when we are under the protection of the Sons of Fergus.' said Naisi. 'Besides you beat me the last time we played chess. I will not lie down on my bed tonight until I have won the game!'

'That pleases me,' returned Deirdre, smiling as though the clashing of swords and the shouts of wounded men were the noise of the cauldron simmering by the fire.

But her heart was beating and her eyes were misting so that she could scarcely distinguish the gold for the silver pieces on the jewelled board.

Conor sent a message to Buino offering him a gift of land and money if he would desert Deirdre and the Sons of Usna. Buino was always dissatisfied and he was sure that in the end, Conor must win. So he ordered his men to cease fighting and went away with them at once, for he dared not stay until Fergus came to hear of his son's treachery.

Then Illan, who could not be bribed, took his sword and, with the few men left, defended the hostel. But the two sons of Conor killed him right before the door.

'This game will never be finished!' cried Naisi, springing up, so that the board was tilted and the shining pieces scattered over the floor.

He seized his weapons and, with Ardan and Ainle beside him, dashed out, surprising Conor's men and killing so many that it seem the hostel might yet be saved.

Then Conor ordered that the hostel should be set on fire. But the Sons of Usna, placing Deirdre in the middle of them, fought on.

'Put a spell upon the Sons of Usna,' Conor implored Cathbad the Druid. 'If I had known how desperate they were, I would have let them stay in Alba. Now we are forced to take them prisoners, but, for the sake of Deirdre, I will not harm them!'

Cathbad believed the king and he wished to put an end to the slaughter, so he made a lake of slime rise about the feet of Deirdre and the three men. When the slime came pouring through the doors of the hostel, Naisi lifted Deirdre up on his shoulder but they could not move and while the four of them stood there helpless, Conor's men seized them and brought them before him.

'This is the most treacherous deed I have known,' cried Cathbad, and he walked out of the hall.

The nobles, looking at Deirdre, would not touch Naisi and his brothers until Owen, Prince of Ferney, envious of their courage, took Naisi's sword from him and with one blow, cut off the heads of the three brothers.

Deirdre covered her face with her hands and would not take them away.

In the morning, Fergus Mac Roy, still flushed with wine, came home to Emain Macha from the feast with Baruch. He found the burning ruins of the Red Branch Hostel, the Sons of Usna slain and with them his son, Illan, while Buino was a traitor. He gazed in horror at Conor and in pity at Deirdre.

'There were two feasts last night, Fergus,' she said. 'You came too late to share ours!'

With a cry of anguish she fell dead beside the bodies of Naisi and his brothers.

Breaking his sword in three, Fergus flung the pieces at the feet of the tyrant and going out of Emain Macha for ever, went to Connaught and offered his arms to Queen Maeve.

Even then Conor would not allow Deirdre to be buried in the one grave with the Sons of Usna. But from their grave and from hers grew two yew trees whose top branches met and entwined with one another so that they could not be parted.

5

LABRA THE MARINER

UGANY the Great, one of the Milesian kings, had two sons, Laery and Corac. Since they were children Leary had been jealous of Corac in games, in learning; in everything, he opposed him. So when Ugany died and Corac was made king in his place, Leary hated him more than ever.

Corac knew of his brother's enmity but, because of their kinship and for the sake of the country, he refused to quarrel. He did not go near him unless he had to and he never went alone.

Laery was always planning to kill his brother and seize the throne. At last Laery sent out a report that he was dead. One of his friends brought a message to Corac asking him to attend the funeral.

Corac forgot all that he had endured from his brother and remembered only the very early days when they were happy together. He went at once to Laery's dun, riding ahead of his warriors with his son, Ailill, and his grandson, a little boy name Maon.

As Corac bent sadly over him, Laery rose suddenly on his elbow and struck Corac dead with a dagger. Leaping up, he snatched a sword and killed Ailill, who was too astonished to defend himself.

Maon ran screaming from the hall, with Laery rushing after him. As Laery seized the child, his screams died and he stood silent. Laery spoke to him but Maon could not answer for he had been struck dumb.

Laery let him go. He wasn't afraid of a dumb child and, before he could change his mind, friends of the dead king

50

hurried Maon away to Munster.

Scoriath, Lord of Fermoy, took the dumb boy into his own home and brought him up with his little daughter, Moraith. Though he could not speak the children understood one another and slowly the horrors which had driven Maon dumb began to grow faint in his mind.

When Maon was almost grown, he was sent to his grandmother's home. She was Kesair, a princess of Gaul, and at her Court the boy was treated with great honour as heir to the throne of Ireland. Yet every day he missed Moraith and repeated to himself his promise to go back to her.

In spite of his silence Maon was well trained and became strong and handsome. While he was growing Moraith was growing too, yet she never forgot the silent boy with his big serious eyes who had followed her everywhere. Now she determined to bring him back and wrote a song reminding Maon of their childhood together and of his promise to return.

She persuaded her father's harper, Craftigny, to set off for Gaul. A ship, loaded with wolfhounds, was sailing there and she gave him her song.

On the ship she sent painted wooden bowls, rings and brooches of beaten silver, studded with river pearls and purple stones.

'Let the princess know we are rich and learned,' she told the harper. 'And remind her that Maon should be a prince in his own country.'

The ship was small and the voyage stormy, so Craftigny was very weary when they landed. But he loved Moraith and he thought of the dumb boy with pity.

'Kind, clever lad,' he said to himself. 'I hope these people of Gaul have been good to him.'

Without resting he travelled to the Court. Maon came at once to welcome him and showed such pleasure the harper was thankful he had come. The timid child he remembered had grown into a tall, fine-looking young man. Though he could not speak, his hearing was so quick he could hear the slightest breeze miles away: his keen eyes were able to see a

51

fish three fathoms under water, and he could keep up easily with a fleet horse for a whole day.

Craftigny noticed Maon's dress—the finest silk; the hilt of his dagger was studded with jewels and when he was riding with the harper, their horses were the swiftest Craftigny had seen.

And all the time Maon's eyes were questioning.

'I wonder now have I the answer to what he daren't ask?' thought the harper.

In the palace that night Craftigny was in the seat of honour beside Kesair. On her other side sat Maon, and the harper could see the great friendship between them.

'Moraith did well to send me,' he thought.

When the dishes were carried away and the jars of wine refilled Kesiar asked Craftigny would he play to them. The boy who carried his harp set it before him and, willingly, the harper drew his fingers along the strings.

Looking at Maon, he sang Moraith's song.

Maon's eyes lit up, his face quivered and he cried out—'Moraith!'

Kesair, the nobles, the serving men and women, stared at the young man with startled looks, for this was the first time he had spoken.

'Moraith!' he said again. 'Moraith has remembered me!'

He stood up and told of Laery's treachery.

'I'll go back!' he cried. 'When I've punished Laery, I'll go to Moraith and thank her for this song. Sing it again, Craftigny!'

Kesair gave him ships and let him choose the warriors to go with him. Craftigny went too and Maon guided the ships. They landed at night, marched secretly to Laery's fort and attacked him before he was awake. Many of Laery's men went over to Maon and before morning came, the traitor was killed and Maon was victorious.

After the battle a druid asked one of Maon's followers who was his leader.

'Loingseach (the Mariner),' replied the man, meaing Maon, who had piloted them from Gaul.

'Can he speak?' asked the druid, wondering if this was Maon grown up.

'He speaks! (Labra),' was the answer. 'But only since he heard the harper's song.'

From that day Maon was called Labra Lynch or Labra the Mariner.

Labra and Craftigny rode down to Munster. They had no need to ride all the way, for Moraith and her father came to meet them. That Labra could speak was as wonderful to her as to him. But when he asked Moraith to marry him, she nodded as if she had become dumb.

Labra's own sufferings made him a good king, except for one terrible deed he committed every year.

Since he had become a man he always wore a hood covering his hair and his hair was long. He had it cut once a year and the man chosen to cut it was put to death immediately after.

One year a young man, the only child of a poor widow, was ordered to cut the king's hair. When he went to the palace, his mother came with him. She wept and begged the king not to kill her son. Whatever was said to her she would not listen. Whatever present was offered to comfort her for her son's loss she refused.

Labra pitied her. He admired her too for she was the first to object to this cruel custom.

'Can your son keep a secret?' he asked.

'As well as any man can!' the widow told him.

'Let your son swear by the Sun and the Wind that he will keep my secret from all men and he shall live.'

The young man took the oath, cut the king's hair and discovered that Labra the Mariner had horse's ears!

He was well paid and went safely home to his mother.

The widow's son kept his promise. The widow was wise and never questioned him. But the strange ears he had seen on the king's head haunted the young man. He dreamed of them: he could think of nothing else. He fell into a fever and his mother, fearing he was dying, went to a druid and told him her trouble.

'It's the secret that's killing him!' said the druid. 'He must tell it! Let him go along the high road which passes your cabin until he comes to the crossroads. Let him take the road going to the right and let him tell his secret to the first tree he meets. Se he will keep his oath yet tell the secret and he will have his health again.

The woman went home joyfully and told her son. He was so weak he could scarcely walk, but he obeyed the druid. He went along the high road till he came to the crossroads. He took the road on the right. It was lined with low-growing bushes and brambles. But he kept on until he came to a pool and there, drooping over the water, was a willow.

The young man put his arms about the tree, laid his head against it and whispered the king's secret. At once the fever left him, his strength returned and he strode home, happy again.

Not many days after Craftigny needed a new harp and went in search of a tree with the proper wood. He strolled along the high road as far as the crossroads, but could not find a tree fine enough. He took the road to the right and was turning back, for bushes and brambles were of no use, when he saw the willow leaning over the pool.

He had it cut down and the new harp was made.

He brought it to the king's hall that night and as he plucked the strings, a voice sang clearly—

Two horse's ears has Labra the Mariner!
Two horse's ears has Labra the Mariner!

Labra frowned, started up, then laughed and, pushing back his hood, showed the horse's ears.

And no man ever again was killed because of this strange happening!

6

CUCHULAIN – THE CHAMPION OF IRELAND

1. The Finding of Setanta

NE summer day, Dectera, a maiden at the Court of Conor Mac Nessa, was playing handball with fifty other girls in the meadow before the Grianan, or women's sun house, when suddenly they all vanished. But fifty-one green and gold butterfies fluttered over the grass and flew off among the trees.

Dectera's mother Maga, her father Cathbad, the Druid, warriors, women of the Court, servants searched for the missing girls. They searched all night and the next day, but found no trace of them. If Dectera alone had disappeared they would have thought her lost for she was dreamy and always wandering. But surely fifty-one girls could not go astray without someone seeing or hearing them. Yet they had passed along no roads, not a traveller had set eye on them; hounds trained in the chase could not pick up their tracks.

'They must be under a spell!' declared Cathbad.

Maga went on looking for her daughter. Three years went by and everyone, except her parents, had forgotten Dectera when one spring morning a flock of birds lighted on the plain around Emain Macha and began to eat the crops. Another flock invaded the orchards until it seemed not an apple would be left on the trees.

Hearing the shouts of the men who were trying to drive away the birds, the king came out from the palace with Fergus Mac Roy and several other nobles. They attacked the thieves with slings. The birds flew a little way, came down again; waited until the hunters drew near then rose in the air once more. All day King Conor and his companions tried to catch up with the birds but could not. Without knowing it they were being brought to the fairy rath of Angus, close by the River Boyne.

When it was too dark to go on, or to find their way back, they searched for shelter but all they could discover was a ruined hut on the river bank.

Conor and a few others wrapped themselves in their cloaks and lay down to sleep. The rest had to make themselves as comfortable as they could on the grass outside. Fergus Mac Roy chose the shelter of a low-growing elder bush. But the leaves were still small and the moonlight shone through the twigs onto his face. He could not sleep. He was too restless to lie still, so he went off quietly and strolled beside the Boyne.

He followed a broad grassy path wondering where it led, when suddenly he saw before him a beautiful building blazing with the light of fires and torches, the gates wide open and the great bronze doors at the top of a flight of wide marble steps were open too.

So surprised he did not think of his crumpled tunic and muddy sandals Fergus strode up the steps and entered the hall.

A young man, taller even than Conor Mac Nessa, for he was Lugh of the Long Arm, was standing in the hall. With him was the lost Dectera and coming through another doorway were the fifty girls who had disappeared with her.

They crowded round Fergus, making him welcome, asking for news from Emain Macha and telling their adventures; of how they had been enticed into the Land of Youth, how happy they were, so happy they would not come back.

In the morning he returned to the hut by the river, but before he reached it, a baby boy was found sleeping there among the warriors. Dectera had lured them to Lugh's fairy palace so that her son might be taken to Conor Mac Nessa's Court and brought up among her own people.

When the king and Fergus Mac Roy returned and the

baby with them, the child was given to Dectera's sister. She took care of him with her own son and he was named Setanta.

2. The Smith's Feast

When Setanta grew old enough he was sent to the Court at Emain Macha where he became one of the Troop of Boys who were trained to be warriors.

There were 150, all sons of chieftains and princes. Soon he became their leader for, from the beginning, Setanta was strong and brave. When King Conor and his nobles were invited to a feast at the fort of Cullen, Setanta was chosen to go with them.

Cullen was a smith, but a smith who made swords and spears for the great warriors. His work was famed throughout Ireland, and, because of his skill and wealth it was indeed an honour for a boy to be invited to his home. Setanta was delighted. But, when the king and his party were starting, the boys were playing hurley. Setanta would never leave a game half finished and played on.

At last the game was ended and Setanta, without resting, went after the chariots. The marks of the wheels and hoofs were clear in the dust of the road so he had no fear of losing his way.

Tossing his ball of crimson leather stuffed tightly with wool, striking it with his caman before it reached the ground, Setanta ran swiftly hoping to hear the chariots. But he was tired when he started. Soon he stopped tossing the ball and no longer ran. The only sounds were the cool evening wind in the trees, the chatter of birds and the splashing of water from rock to rock.

'Who would have thought they'd be so far ahead,' he thought. 'But I had to play the game out.'

The road dwindled to a path as it entered the forest. The treetops were still tipped with light, but among the trees Setanta moved in shadow. His eyes were keen and he could see the track lying white before him.

Branches rubbed and creaked, there was a continual crackling of twigs and, among the undergrowth, savage calls and terrifying snarls.

'Maybe I should have gone with the chariots,' thought Setanta. 'But how could I, not knowing who had won?'

He moved carefully and, as he glanced over his right shoulder, flaming eyes glared at him between two tree trunks. He stared back in terror. Suddenly the eyes were no longer there and he hurried on.

He heard the patter of feet on the path behind him and tried to run. But he was too weary and instead he forced himself to look back. The moon was rising and a shaft of light pierced the trees. The wind was blowing a scatter of leaves along the path. They danced a little way then piled up quivering. Farther on other leaves swirled in a circle.

'Aren't I very foolish to be afraid of dried leaves!' Setanta murmured.

The forest was thinning, for the path crossed the narrow end. The boy listened to the tap-tap of his soft leather sandals and the sound was like a companion.

He came out from the trees. Bushes grew up from a sea of grass and Setanta went by a wild heath silvered with moonlight. The scufflings of little animals, sleepy complaints from overcrowded nests and the trickling of hidden streams were all about him.

Setanta had never been to Cullen's fort before and he watched anxiously for a light or the sound of voices. He was sure he had come the right way and he heard the smith lived barely two spear throws beyond the forest.

The ground was rising. He paused as a howl came on the wind.

Was it a wolf? Even a solitary warrior might fear a wolf and Setanta had no arms, only his hurley stick.

The howl came again.

That's no wolf, but a dog!' decided the boy. 'Cullen's watch dog. I must be nearly there.'

The path topped the crest and once more widened to a

road. On the next ridge Setanta saw a red glow against the darkened sky. He had reached the fort of Cullen.

3. *The Hound of Cullen*

Like most of the forts of that day Cullen's home was surrounded by a bank of beaten earth with a stone wall set on top. A wide wooden gate closed at sunset and opened at daybreak was the only entrance. Inside around the one-storied buildings was space for all the cattle which were driven in each night. Most forts were guarded by armed men. Cullen kept no men at his gate. The only guard was an enormous Irish wolf hound. 'With him at my gate,' boasted the smith, 'I fear nothing but an army.'

Setanta's feet were aching as he climbed the hill. He could hear music and laughing shouts from the banquet hall and longed to be there. He reached the huge closed gates, but no voice challenged him.

Was the guard sleeping?

Setanta was shivering in the cold night air. His last meal was so many hours back he could not remember what he had eaten. He lifted his caman to beat on the gate and opened his mouth to shout when he heard growling and snuffling so close he leaped away. Something was moving inside the wall. Cullen kept no guard at his gate—only his wolf hound!

Setanta had heard and forgotten.

'No hound shall keep me outside till morning!' he declared, and gripping his caman in his teeth, he leaped at the gate, caught the top by the tips of his fingers, hauled himself up and crouched there.

In the moonlight he saw a great beast gazing at him, eyes gleaming, fangs showing. A queer whimper came from its jaws, then a howl of anger. Springing it reached for the boy with its powerful claws.

As the hound sprang up, Setanta jumped down. He thrust at it with the curved stick, which was broken in two with one snap of the sharp teeth. Head outstretched it rushed at the boy. Setanta dodged, flung out his hands and caught the brute by the throat. As they wrestled, the hound snarling, Setanta panting, the doors of the hall were flung open and men carrying torches swarmed out, the king and his companions with them.

Through the crowd burst a tall, broad man—Cullen, the Smith.

'Let go!' he shouted. 'Let go!' and rushed to save the stranger.

With a last effort Setanta gripped the hound by its fore-legs, raised it above his head and flung it crashing to the ground. He heard a muffled growl, then the great head fell sideways. Placing his foot upon the lifeless body, Setanta turned and faced them all.

'By my sword!' cried King Conor. 'I am proud to have this lad in my Corps. The size of him and of that huge hound!'

Setanta listened to the praise with sparkling eyes until he noticed the Smith standing silently with bent head. Then he understood what he had done. He touched Cullen's hand.

'I killed the hound to save my own life. But I should have stayed outside,' he said. 'I had no right to enter.'

'He was my friend,' sighed the Smith. 'He died for the safe-keeping of this dun and he will never guard it again.'

Now there were tears of shame in Setanta's eyes.

'If I could give back the life I have taken, I would,' he told Cullen. 'But give me a pup of this hound and I'll train him to be the equal of his sire. Until them I'll be your hound and I'll guard this fort!'

And from the day Setanta was known as Cuchulain—the Hound of Cullen.

4. The Promise of Emer

One day Cuchulain heard Cathbad, the Druid, saying that the youth who was given the weapons of a man before

61

nightfall would become one of the most famous warriors in Ireland, but his life would be short and dangersous.

Young Cuchulain went straight before the king and demanded the arms of manhood. Conor smiled, for Cuchulain was small and slight, but handed the boy two full-sized spears. Cuchulain snapped the hafts in pieces between his fingers. Two stronger spears were brought, but he broke them in the same way and went on destroying weapons until Conor sent for a sword and spear of his own. These Cuchulain could not break.

With the weapons the king gave him a war chariot and told him to choose horses from the royal stables.

At this time Emer, daughter of Forgall, lord of Lusca, was the most beautiful girl in Ireland. Cuchulain loved her the moment he set eyes on her at the Court and now that he had a warrior's weapons and chariot he thought he had every right to ask her to marry him.

He set off in his new chariot with Laeg, his friend and charioteer to Dun Forgall, where the village of Lusk now stands. Cuchulain was proud as they drew up at the gate. Forgall was away so it was Emer who welcomed them.

Cuchulain was quick and dark, gentle and well taught. His crimson cloak with its many coloured edging was fastened with a brooch of gold and the shield on his back was crimson too with a rim of beaten gold. He laid down his weapons and at once asked Emer to marry him. She liked him better than any of the young men in her father's dun, but she shook her head.

'It is lucky my father is not here,' she said. 'He would tell you I must marry a man of his choice. And he hasn't chosen you. He intends me to marry a king. But if you were a hero, Cuchulain, a champion of Ireland, then I would choose you. That I promise!'

Cuchulain picked up his sword and spear.

'When I come again, Emer,' he replied, 'I will be the proudest champion in Ireland!'

Away he drove with his red-haired charioteer Laeg and back to Emain Macha, to begin his training as a champion.

62

In those days champions were trained by women warriors and as the most famous of these was Scatha of the Land of Shadows, Cuchulain went in search of her.

Everyone had heard of her, but no one could tell him where she lived. He travelled through Ireland, through forests and over bogs. At every Dun, at every fort he asked for news of Scatha. Not until he reached the northernmost point did he meet one who could show him the way.

An old man, too feeble to fish or hunt, sat in the sun against a rock above the sea and pointed a trembling finger to where Alba lay across the waves.

'Take my boat. I am too old to use it now. It lies on the sand at the foot of this rock. Go straight over. Then keep north. You will come to dark forests, you will pass over desolate moors. There are swift rivers you must ford. There will be rain and cold and mist, always mist. You will come where sea and land are so mingled you would need the wings of a bird to go safely. Then an island of cliffs will loom dimly from the waves and that will be the land you are seeking—the Land of Shadows. I have known many who came this way asking for Scatha. Maybe they found her. They did not return. May you be more fortunate, noble youth.'

The old man's boat was a skin curragh so light it slid over the waves without taking in a drop of water. Cuchulain, brave on land, shuddered when the curragh balanced for an instant on the crest of a wave, then swept into a green hollow, only to be tossed so high it seemed he could touch the clouds.

When he reached the Alban shore he could scarcely walk. But, too impatient to rest, he turned north in search of Scatha.

5. *The Training of a Champion*

This was wilder country than Cuchulain had seen before. Rocks piled on rocks; cliffs, precipices with waterfalls;

surging streams and sudden lakes: all so savage he thought the forests a protection until he heard the wolves. The inhabitants he encountered, though wild and sullen, were hospitable. There were others, never seen, who shot arrows at him if he stopped to make sure of his path, flung spears as he crept along narrow shelves and hurled rocks to cast him from his scanty foothold.

He was forced to make long journeys inland to cross rivers or arms of the sea which stretched for miles into the mountains. When he asked for Scatha or the Land of Shadows the people shook their heads and looked at him in wonder. A few advised him to turn back. His sandals were in holes, his tunic in rags but he persevered until he came to the Plain of Ill-luck. Then indeed he was discouraged.

The great bog stretched before him. He could not see the slightest trace of a path and pools of dark water surrounded any rock that rose from the desolation. There were neither flowers, nor grass and no birds sang there.

'Have I been foolish to dream of finding Scatha when only one old man could tell me of her?' he thought. 'Should I turn back while I can?'

As he stood lonely and hesitating, across the quaking bog, treading lightly and surely, came a young man with shining hair and sparkling eyes, whose friendly smile made Cuchulain forget his doubts.

Under his arm he carried a flaming wheel.

'Take this,' he said, 'and do not fear to follow it. When you come to the Perilous Glen this apple will show you the safe way.' He put the wheel into Cuchulain's left hand and a golden apple into the right, then sped off as if his feet were winged.

Cuchulain stared after him until he was only a gleaming blur in the distance.

'Can he be Lugh of the Long Arm?' wondered Cuchulain. 'But why should an Immortal help me?'

He did not know that Lugh was really his father.

His courage returned as he set the wheel rolling over the quaking mud. It blazed with light and the heat from it made a firm path on which Cuchulain walked securely.

As he reached the other side the flaming wheel rolled out of sight and the wanderer stood gazing into a dark wooded glen from which rose the howls and snarls of savage beasts.

There was no way round so Cuchulain tossed the golden apple before him. It landed on a high narrow ridge of rock and, springing down on it, he stepped carefully, trying not to hear the appalling sounds coming up from the depths of the Perilous Glen.

The ridge widened as it climbed above the trees and led Cuchulain to an open meadow.

After the lonely days since he had left Ireland Cuchulain was thrilled to see a group of lads and young men playing hurley. They dropped their sticks and crowded round him.

Cuchulain discovered that they had come to learn the arts of war from Scatha and that several were from Ireland. One Ferdia, son of the Firbolg, Daman, became his friend and while they were training to be champions they were never parted.

But Cuchulain could not believe he had really arrived at the end of his search.

'Where is Scatha's dun?' he asked. 'I heard she lived on an island called the Land of Shadows.'

Ferdia pointed.

'There is the Land of Shadows and yonder is the dun of Scatha.

Beyond the sunny meadow the land rose in rock terraces which ended in a cliff. Far below the sea surged in a long winding channel. A swirling mist hung over it and on the other side an island of grey dripping rocks towered to the sky. As Cuchulain gazed he made out the dun perched far up, a grim terrifying dwelling. He could see it but faintly for it was shrouded in mist and shadows.

'How can I reach it?' asked Cuchulain.

'You must wait!' Ferdia told him. 'This is our training ground. There is our hall. Tomorrow you will meet Scatha here and she will test you. She does not train all who come to her.'

'I have journeyed so far,' protested Cuchulain. 'Is there no way of coming to her?'

'Look!' said Ferdia. 'There is the Bridge of Leaps and only Scatha can cross it, for the two last feats she teaches her chosen champions are the leap across the bridge and the thrust of the Gae Bolg.'

Cuchulain saw what seemed to be a thin curved plank suspended from cliff to cliff.

'If you step upon one end of that bridge the middle rises and flings you back,' explained Ferdia. 'And if you jump it's so slippery you'll miss your footing and fall into the gulf where the sea monsters are lurking.'

'The bridge is there to be crossed. I will cross it!' declared Cuchulain.

Ferdia persuaded him to bathe and rest at the hall. He was given new sandals and fresh clothing and sat with the others at their evening meal.

The road to the bridge was steep and winding. Cuchulain had forgotten his weariness and while his companions still lingered at the table he started alone.

When he reached the top he looked down and Ferdia raised his hand.

Cuchulain ran at the bridge and, with a flying leap, tried to land upon the middle. It lifted under him and he was tossed back. He could hear shouts from the meadow, some encouraging, some jeering, and tried again.

The fourth time he landed in the centre of the bridge, sprang forward and stood on the Island of Shadows.

He strode on until he reached the dun and there was Scatha in the entrance coming to meet him.

She was so tall Cuchulain did not reach to her shoulder. Her black hair was bound about her head like a shining helmet and her grey eyes stabbed Cuchulain's as if they were twin blades of steel.

She had watched from the dun and was so pleased with Cuchulain's strength and perseverance that she made him her pupil without further test.

Scáta

Cuchulain stayed with her for a year and a day learning all she could teach him. Often she boasted of his skill for, except Ferdia, she had never known a young man so easy to teach and so eager for all the knowledge she could give.

They fought with her in the wars among the tribes and several times the three of them turned defeat into victory. Scatha felt sad when the time came for them to go back to their own country.

On the last day she taught Cuchulain the use of the Gae Bolg or body spear and gave her own to him for he was the first untried champion she thought worthy to use it. This terrible spear was thrown with the foot and if it entered a warrior's body it filled every limb with its barbs.

Cuchulain said farewell and, at the last moment, he and Ferdia renewed their vows of friendship and promised to help one another as long as they lived.

6. Champion of Ireland

The evening following his return Cuchulain wandered along the shore of the Grey lake thinking of his training with Scatha, his friendship with Ferdia and the promise Emer had made before he went away.

He stopped to watch a faint mist which rose from the centre of the lake and turned into a shimmering cloud. Slowly it drifted to the marshy bank, growing denser until a great grey stallion, so perfect Cuchulain gasped in joy, stepped daintily to the path.

Suddenly Cuchulain sprang on the horse's back and gripping its body with his knees, twisted his hands in the thick flowing mane. Rearing it tried to throw him, but Cuchulain clung on. It raced round and round the lake, rising on its hind legs, then flinging down on its head only to jump with all four feet into the air in an effort to toss its rider. Both were covered with foam and sweat and Cuchulain felt he could hold on no longer when the stallion dropped to a gentle canter and whinnied in submission. From the glen before them came an answering whinny; a coal black steed galloped up and trotted beside the grey.

Cuchulain brought them home and Laeg, his charioteer, harnessed them to the war chariot. Laeg was the finest charioteer in the country; the Grey of Macha, and the Black Steed of the Glen were the best horses and the three of them stayed with Cuchulain to the last day of his life.

Back in his home at Dun Dalgan, now Dundalk, Cuchulain drove in his chariot with the new horses to the highest of the Mountains of Mourne and looked over the land of Ulster. He turned south and gazed across the Plain of Bregia where Tara and Teltin, and Brugh na Boyna lay. Laeg told him the names of all the hills and duns they could see and many beyond their sight.

'Over yonder is the great dun of the sons of Nechtan,' said Laeg.

'Are they the sons of Nechtan who are said to have killed more Ulstermen than are now living on the earth?' asked Cuchulain.

'I have heard that said,' replied Laeg.

'Then drive to the dun of the sons of Nechtan!' ordered Cuchulain.

So they drove to the fort. Before the gate they found a pillar stone and round it a collar of bronze ornamented with writing in Ogham signs—

'Any many of age to bear arms who reads this stone shall hold himself under *geis* (in honour bound) not to depart without challenging one of the dwellers of this dun to single combat.'

Cuchulain put his arms about the stone. Pushing and heaving he tugged it out of the earth and flung it into the river below.

'You must be looking for a violent death!' exclaimed Laeg.

Foill, son of Nechtan, hearing the crash and the splashing, came out from the gate of the dun. When he saw Cuchulain he thought he was only a boy and threatened him with his fists.

Cuchulain called to him to bring his weapons for he would not slay an unarmed man.

'You can't kill Foill!' declared Laeg. 'He is protected by magic against the point or edge of any blade.'

'I'm glad you told me that,' said Cuchulain as Foill came out from the dun once more, armed, but without a shield for he did not think he needed one. He could not take Cuchulain seriously as a fighter.

As Foill rushed upon him with his great sword uplifted Cuchulain put a ball of iron in his sling and hurled it at the warrior so that it went right through his head. So fierce was his rush that Foill still came on and Cuchulain had to spring aside while the body of his enemy went on and crashed down the bank into the river.

The other sons of Nechtan came hurrying out. Cuchulain fought and killed them one by one. Ordering everyone out of the dun he set it on fire and drove away leaving it blazing behind.

A flock of wild geese flew overhead, keeping up with his horses. Cuchulain brought sixteen of them down alive with his sling and tied them loosely to his chariot so that their fluttering wings excited the horses until they galloped madly across the plain.

A herd of deer broke from cover and raced before them. Even the Grey of Macha and the Black Steed of the Glen could not come up with them. Cuchulain leaped from the chariot and chasing after the deer on foot caught two great stags which he harnessed to the chariot with ropes and so arrived in triumph at the banqueting hall of Emain Macha.

About this time there was a chieftain known as Briccriu of the Poisoned Tongue because he made mischief wherever he was. Now he started the warriors arguing as to who was champion of Erin. It was decided that the three bravest were—

Laery the Triumphant,
Conall the Victorious,
Cuchulain.

But which of these should be entitled to the Champion's

Portion at a feast could not be agreed.

To prevent a deadly quarrel a demon named The Terrible was called from the lake where he dwelt and asked to decide.

He told them that anyone who wished to be known as the Champion of Erin could chop off his head today. But then the would-be Champion must lay his own head on the block tomorrow.

The warriors looked at one another in horror. Only Cuchulain was willing to face the test. Drawing his sword he struck off the head of the demon, who jumped up, seized his head and sprang with it into the lake.

The next morning, the demon, his head back on his shoulders, appeared among them. Cuchulain trembled, yet he kept his promise and laid his head on the block. The demon swung his axe—once, twice, three times—then struck the block with the back of the axe and cried—

'Arise, Cuchulain, Champion of Ireland!'

Now Cuchulain felt he could go to Emer and ask her to keep her promise. He knew her father Forgall the Wily was opposed to him. He sent a message warning her to be ready, ordered his war chariot and beneath the shields and weapons concealed rugs and cushions.

Laeg halted the chariot before Forgall's dun and, while the guards at the gate challenged them, Cuchulain leaped 'the hero's salmon leap', which Scatha had taught him, over the high ramparts of the dun.

Emer and her foster sisters were ready, wearing their grandest clothes and all their jewels. Protecting them with his shield Cuchulain fought a way to the gate. As the girls climbed into the chariot Forgall and his sons returned from a foray. Before they realised what had happened Laeg shouted to his horses and they bounded forward. Forgall followed with all the chariots and horses he possessed. But he had none equal to the Grey of Macha and the Black Steed of the Glen, nor charioteer the equal of Laeg. So Emer was brought in safety to Emain Macha.

Conor Mac Nessa loved splendour and he had the marriage of Emer and Cuchulain celebrated with such grandeur that even Maeve of Connaught was envious. A banquet was held lasting for days. The doors of the great hall were flung open so that no one who came need go away fasting. There were hurling and wrestling matches, tournaments of all kinds of fighting, displays of strength and skill. There were storytellers and harpers, who never told the same story, or played the same tune twice. Even when Emer and Cuchulain drove off to his dun at Dun Dalgan the feasting went on. They looked back and Emer saw the glow of fires flung against the dark sky and heard singing and music. But Cuchulain heard only the clash of arms and the cries of combat.

7. *The Cattle Raid of Cooley, or the Tain Bo Cuailgne*

Conor Mac Nessa reigned in Ulster—Maeve and Ailell ruled in Connaught. From their palace of Cruachan they could look over the plain of Mag Ai and the ruins of that great palace are there in Roscommon to this day.

Ailell was a boastful, easy-going man. Maeve was proud— proud of her titles, Queen of Connaught, Maeve of Fal; proud of her father, the Ard Righ (High King) living at Tara, proud of her wealth and power.

Ailell bragged of his fighting men.

'I have 3,000 well-trained, well-armed young men to protect me. Not a noisy rabble!' declared Maeve.

'I have more horses, serving men and maids than anyone in Ireland, even yourself!' Ailell taunted her.

All night they sat, matching their chariots and horses, the shields and weapons of their warriors, the number of their servants, their clothes and jewels, their flocks of sheep and herds of swine, even the cauldrons and spits in their kitchens. They had as much and no more than one another.

Maeve's eyes were closing with sleep when she remembered Finnbenach (the white-horned), her red bull with white horns. Ailell had nothing to compare with it.

In the morning she ordered her steward, Mac Roth, to bring the wonderful bull that she might display it to the king.

Along came the huge beast, tossing its white horns and walking as proudly as Maeve herself.

'Have you a bull to equal mine?' she asked.

'I have not!' replied Ailell. 'But haven't you noticed it is my herd it leads, not yours? Hasn't Mac Roth told you—it will not stay in the herd belonging to a woman, even if she is Maeve of Connaught!'

Maeve was furious. She turned to the steward, her green eyes flashing, her long pale face flushed with anger.

'Is there such another bull in Ireland?' she demanded.

'There is indeed!' replied Mac Roth. 'The Brown Bull Donn of Cooley, that is owned by Dara, son of Fachtna in Uladh, is the noblest bull in Ireland.'

Then Maeve was no longer troubled that Finnbenach had deserted her herd. She longed for the Brown Bull of Cooley more than anything else in the world.

'Go to Dara,' she told Mac Roth. 'Tell him Maeve of Connaught asks the loan of the Brown Bull for one year. I will give back the bull and fifty heifers with him. If Dara will not be parted from his bull and would live here in Connaught, he shall have as much land as ever he possessed in Ulster, a royal chariot and my friendship.'

Dara was delighted with the offer. He had heard of the splendour of Maeve's Court and her offer was generous. But her messengers foolishly boasted that if their mistress's wish was not granted, she and Ailell would take the bull by force.'

'Let them come if they dare!' cried Dara, and sent back and answer of defiance.

His rath was in Cooley, between Dundalk Bay and lovely Carlingford Lough, on a height near Warrenpoint, just across the Ulster border.

He was a friendly man and though he was sorry to refuse Maeve, his anger had been roused. His friends in Ulster were far better pleased with his refusal than if he had gone into

Connaught with the famous Donn. They did not know how determined Maeve was to take it from them.

'If Dara won't lend his bull, there's nothing to be done but raid for it,' she told Ailell, and sent heralds throughout Connaught to summon her hosts.

'This shall be the biggest raid in the history of Connaught!' declared Maeve, and went to her chief Druid to ask what would be her fortune in the fight.

'Among those who will stay behind in peace and those who go into the war there is none dearer to us than ourselves,' said Maeve. 'Tell me our fate. Shall we come alive out of this raid?'

'Who comes or comes not back in safety, you shall come,' said the Druid.

As they returned, her charioteer swung the horses to the right so that they should carry the good omen with them. But they were only half-way to Cruachan when, standing before them right up against the horses, Maeve saw a young girl with long fair hair, dressed in green and with a shuttle of gold she wove a web upon a loom.

'Who are you?' cried Maeve, startled by the girl's sudden appearance. 'And what are you weaving?'

'I am the prophetess Fedelma from the Fairy Mound of Croghan,' replied the girl. 'I am weaving the four provinces of Ireland together for the raid.'

'Can you see our host in the battle?' asked Maeve eagerly.

'I see them all red,' replied Fedelma.

'Yet there is not one of the Ultonian warriors can lift a spear against us,' said the queen, 'for the Curse of Macha is upon them.'

'I see your host all red!' repeated the girl. 'I see one man against them—slender, young, gentle, but in battle a hero and his name is Cuchulain!'

Fedelma vanished and Maeve drove on to Rath Croghan wondering.

Long ago, because of a great wrong done to her by the warriors of Ulster, Queen Macha had laid a curse upon them that, for generations, in the hour of their greatest peril,

74

they should lie stricken and helpless. This was the Debility of the Ultonians. But because Cuchulain was the son of Lugh, a god, he was not affected.

At dawn the great army started on the march for Ulster. Fergus Mac Roy, who came from the North, led the host and kept a watch for Cuchulain.

All the champion could hope was to delay the invaders until the Ultonians had recovered. He went into the forest and, standing on one leg, using only one hand and closing one eye, he cut an oak sapling and twisted it into a circle. On this he cut in Ogham letters how the circle was made and put the host of Maeve under *geis* not to pass by for twelve hours unless one of them had, in the same way, made a similar circlet.

He put the circlet round the pillar stone of Ardcullin and went back to the mountains.

When Maeve and her army came to Ardcullin, they found the circlet and its message. They knew they must do the Champion's bidding or great evil would come upon them. There wasn't one of them could imitate Cuchulain's feat, so they camped there for the night. A heavy snow storm swept over them, their tents and cooking pots were far behind and they spent many wretched hours. But in the morning they marched over the whitened plain into Ulster.

Cuchulain kept ahead and hiding among the rocks, saw two chariots sent on by Maeve to give warning of any unexpected enemy. As he came out the warriors rushed at him with uplifted swords but he killed them both and their drivers too.

With one stroke of his sword he cut down a forked tree and drove it deep into the ford, now called Athgowla or the Ford of the Forked Pole, where Maeve must pass. On each prong he placed a head. The army came marching along, but halted when they saw this terrible sight. The tree with its gory burden blocked the ford and no chariot could pass until it had been taken away.

First one man, then two tugged at the tree. It was planted so deeply they could not move it an inch. A rope was tied about it and fastened to a chariot. Not until late that night and after seventeen chariots had been broken in the struggle, could they tear out the tree!

Next day Cuchulain, still watching, heard the sound of an axe felling trees. Going into the forest he found one of the Connaught men cutting chariot poles of holly.

'We have damaged our chariots in chasing that famous deer, Cuchulain,' he explained. 'My master, Orlam, is proud of his chariots.'

'Shall I help you?' asked Cuchulain.

'If you could trim the poles as I cut them, I'd be thankful,' replied the man.

Taking the long straight branches at the top, Cuchulain drew them against the set of twigs through his toes. Then ran his fingers down them.

'There you are!' he said.

The man stared at the poles, smooth and shining as though they had been planed and polished.

'I've never seen that job done better,' he said. 'Yet I do not think this is your proper work. Who are you?'

'I am Cuchulain!' said the Champion.

The Connaught man stared doubtfully. The hero was small and slight. He had chatted and laughed as they worked together. Now he stood straight, his eyes blazed and that hero light which shone about his head in battle quivered like a flame.

The man trembled and dropped his axe.

'Don't be afraid. I never harm messengers, nor unarmed men,' Cuchulain told him. 'Run now and tell your master Orlam, that Cuchulain is on his way.'

Forgetting his axe, the man rushed from the forest but Cuchulain raced him and meeting Orlam first, cut off his head. Maeve saw him a moment as he waved this trophy of war upon the hillside. Then he vanished in the mist. Cuchulain was alone and the great Western army seemed very secure in its camp. But he did not leave them in peace for an hour. Across a narrow pass leading to the Plain of the Swinherd, he flung an oak and placed a *geis* upon it so that until one of the chiefs should leap this in his chariot, the army must not go by.

Thirty made the attempt; thirty horses fell and thirty chariots were smashed before Fergus Mac Roy leaped clear over the oak.

As Maeve sat outside her tent looking on at two men wrestling, a stone from an unseen sling killed a tame bird sitting on her shoulder and as she started in surprise, another struck the pet squirrel from her knee.

Men dared not leave the camp alone. Even when they were in twos and threes, Cuchulain attacked and killed them. Daring young fighters, longing to gain fame, went in search of him and did not return. Camp followers became afraid to seek plunder unless they went in bands of twenty or thirty.

'He has but one body!' cried Maeve indignantly. 'Let but a tried champion go against him!'

She tried to persuade Fergus Mac Roy to challenge Cuchulain. But Fergus would not. He would lead the army of Maeve and Ailell against the Ultonian army. But he would not attack Cuchulain whom he had known as a boy when they were both at Emain Macha.

One moonlit night Cuchulain looked down on the camp from a height and every time a face showed white, he used his sling. Men, half-asleep, heard groans around them but thought they were dreaming. In the morning a hundred warriors lay dead.

Maeve now sent a messenger to Cuchulain offering him wealth and land if he would desert the Ultonians. They were curious to see one another and talked across a deep, narrow stream. Maeve had seen the hero in his battle frenzy, his eyes protruding, his muscles swollen, the red light flaming upward from his head. Now she saw a slim, boyish man, who would not swerve from his allegiance to Ulster if she gave him the half of Connaught.

Cuchulain had seen Maeve only from a distance. Now he looked upon her proud beauty, her yellow hair falling like a cloak around her, her green eyes, her pale face. Her rich

clothes and wonderful jewels, her splendid chariot with restless, stamping horses, made him realise the grandeur of her Court. He knew her courage and that she was the cleverest ruler in Ireland.

'Yet, she'd risk everything for the sake of a brown bull!' he thought.

At last Fergus Mac Roy persuaded Cuchulain not to harry Maeve's army if they would send only one warrior at a time against him. While they fought, the army could march. But when one was victorious, they must camp until the next day.

'Better to lose one man each day than a hundred each night,' said Maeve.

The single combats began at the Ford of Dee, now called Ardee.

In his lonely camp Cuchulain practised the feats Scatha had taught him and played chess with Laeg, his charioteer. Day by day young chieftains from Maeve's army, came out to challenge him and Cuchulain was always the victor.

Soon it was hard to find warriors worthy to fight the Champion and Maeve began to regret the treaty she had made.

She sent back to Connaught for Natchrantal, a chief famous for his size and skill with arms. When he came and saw the Ulster champion he was very scornful.

'He is only a boy and yet you are afraid of him. I thought better of Maeve's warriors!'

He refused to take shield or sword but carried only a few light spears.

Natchrantal came upon Cuchulain fowling on the lake below his camp and, without warning, cast one of his spears. Cuchulain jumped to one side and, as the blade struck the ground, took aim with his sling at a waterfowl. Each time Natchrantal cast a spear Cuchulain sent a shot after a bird. At the seventh cast a flock of birds rose from the water and Cuchulain followed them out of sight.

Back at the royal camp Natchrantal told what had happened.

'I knew it!' cried Maeve. 'He can fight young lads, but he flies from a seasoned warrior.'

'You are wrong!' declared Fergus Mac Roy. 'Cuchulain will not fight any but fully armed men. Let Natchrantal go tomorrow fully armed and he will find Cuchulain ready to meet him.'

When Natchrantal went out the following day, carrying shield and sword and his heavy spears, he found Cuchulain waiting on the mountainside. Yet still he could not believe that this quiet young man was a great champion.

'Are you indeed Cuchulain?' he shouted.

Cuchulain waved his hand.

'You will find the man you seek down yonder glen.'

As Natchrantal strode off, Cuchulain rubbed blackberry juice on his face to pretend he had a beard.

'If fools judge by appearance we must let them have their way,' he said to Laeg, laughing.

And he raced after Natchrantal.

The Connaught man heard the jangle of arms and swung round.

'I heard you were looking for me,' said Cuchulain.

'Are you Cuchulain?' asked Natchrantal.

'I am, and I will give you choice of arms though you are the challenger.'

'I choose spears!' replied Natchrantal, throwing his spear.

As it whistled through the air Cuchulain leaped over it.

'Now do the same with mine!' he said.

He flung his so high even he himslf could not have leaped over it, yet so quickly and surely that the spear came straight down upon Natchrantal, piercing his head.

'I am indeed slain by the Champion of Ireland!' he said, as he fell dead.

While they fought, a third of Maeve's army made a sudden march through Ulster, burning and plundering. The Brown Bull had taken refuge with a herd of cows in a glen at Slievegullion in Armagh. The amazed raiders found Donn of Cooley there and drove him off in triumph. Cuchulain watched their return and hurried down to meet them. He attacked and killed the leader, a fair-haired man named Buic, son of Banblai. But the raiders drove the herd on and he could not stop them.

Maeve watched their coming with delight.

'Now I have defeated Cuchulain and the Cattle Raid of Cooley is ended!' she said.

8. At the Ford

Maeve was wrong. She was satisfied. She had captured the Brown Bull and Ailell could not boast that he held the finest bull in the country, for Finnbenach and Donn Cooley were equally strong, fearless and handsome. But Maeve had started a war and every day came allies from the South and West, eager for a share of the fighting and plunder, while Cuchulain was still the solitary champion of Ulster.

He sat beside his half-dead fire with his head in his hands, feeling lonely and defeated, and weary of fighting. If only he could have won back the Brown Bull he would have been strong and tireless. Now he wondered how long this terrible, senseless war would last.

A golden light fell across his face and, looking up, he saw coming by Maeve's encampment, the young man who had helped him when he was on the road to Scatha's dwelling. He would have jumped to his feet in respect but a powerful hand pressed him down and he sank back too weary to resist.

'Sleep softly, Cuchulain, and I will watch here with you.'

Then Cuchulain slept and dreamed while a voice sang softly above him—

> Sleep hero while the god of light
> Watches your foes throughout the night,
> And dream of finer battles far
> Than this vain Raid of Cooley.
>
> Ferdia shall die; Cuchulain too:
> The boys of Ulster fade like dew.
> Yet Maeve shall lose, although she wins
> This Cattle Raid of Cooley.

The hosts of Maeve saw on the mountain the golden light which surrounded Lugh and they were afraid.

At Emain Macha the warriors still lay ill and helpless. Only grown men suffered from the Curse and when the boys who were trained there, heard of Cuchulain's desperate struggle, they put on their light armour, took their spears and with King Conor's young son, Follaman, leading them, marched southward.

'I will never go home until I carry with me the diadem of Ailell's!' he declared.

Not one of them returned. Three times the 150 young heroes attacked Maeve's army. Three times their own number were killed. But in the end they were overcome.

Cuchulain slept for three days and nights. When he awoke, fresh and ready for battle, he feared the invaders might have passed on without check or challenge.

Lugh told him how the boy corps from Emain Macha had taken his place.

'How many live?' asked Cuchulain quietly.

'Not one!' answered Lugh. 'Conor's son led them. They fought and died like warriors.'

'And I slept while they were fighting for me!' cried the Champion. 'But I'll avenge them.'

The battle fury came on him. He leapt into his chariot and, with Laeg beside him drove the Grey of Macha and the Black Steed of the Glen. Round and round Maeve's camp they thundered, ploughing the earth until it rose into ramparts. The scythes upon the wheels caught the bodies of the crowded host so that they were piled in a wall. Cuchulain shouted and all the demons and goblins in Erin answered back. The army was panic-stricken and men, rushing about in terror, fought one another while many died from horror and fear.

This was called the Carnage of Murthemney.

Now the Clan Catalin came against Cuchulain. Catalin was a wizard who considered himself and his twenty-seven sons as one person. What one did they all did and their weapons were so poisonous that a man lightly grazed by one would die in nine days. When the Clan met Cuchulain each threw a spear. Cuchulain caught the twenty-eight spears on his shield and drew his sword to cut them off. Clan Catalin rushed upon him, flung him down and forced his face into the stony earth.

Fiacha from Ulster, who was with Maeve's host, could not bear this unequal fight. Rushing forward he cut off the twenty-eight hands with one stroke and Cuchulain, staggering to his feet, destroyed the whole Clan. So, luckily, there was no one left to tell Maeve what Fiacha had done.

Ferdia, Cuchulain's old comrade, was fighting for Maeve. But though she asked him again and again to challenge Cuchulain, he refused.

She taunted him and threatened that the rhymers would make ballads against him and years after his death they would still be sung.

But if he would go out against the Champion, her daughter, the lovely Finnavair, would be his wife, and lands and great wealth would be his.

Then Ferdia went, slowly and unwillingly. He had never forgotten his friendship with Cuchulain. Although he was on the other side he was proud of his friend's great skill and courage, and gloried in his exploits.

'If we had stayed together, not even Maeve and all her army could have beaten us!' he thought.

Ferdia drove to the ford before the sun had risen and while the river was still hidden in mist. He lay in his chariot, dreaming of their early years together and wondering which of them should die, for he was sure that when he and Cuchulain met, only one of them would depart alive.

Not until dawn did he hear the Champion's chariot approaching. The two friends looked at one another across the ford.

'I did not expect you, Ferdia, to come to do battle with me,' said Cuchulain. 'When we were with Scatha we shared feast and fight; we shared one bed and where you went, I went with you. In those days I would not have believed that my friend Ferdia would live to challenge me!'

'It must be!' replied Ferdia. 'Forget our old comradeship, Hound of Ulster! My hand is the one that shall wound you. Choose your weapons!'

'You have the first choice!' Cuchulain told him.

They began with javelins and they were so well matched that the weapons darted backwards and forwards across the river without once drawing blood.

Cuchulain smiled. But they were warriors and Maeve's army watched from a distance.

When the sun was overhead they began casting their heavy spears and though both were wounded, there was nothing to choose between them. They might have been back with Scatha practising in the Land of Shadows.

Evening came. They flung down their weapons and Cuchulain rushed into the ford to go to Ferdia. But Ferdia met him halfway. They clasped hands, then sat by the same fire, talking of long ago. All that they had of healing ointment and food and drink they shared, and when they lay down on their beds of green rushes they almost forgot the war which had brought them there.

Next day they continued to fight. All day they thrust and slashed and, when night came, they were so weary and covered with wounds they ceased the combat without a word.

But once more they were friends.

In the morning Cuchulain, aching all over, looked at Ferdia and saw his pale face and dimmed eyes.

'Turn back, Ferdia!' he said. 'Let the fight be over or it will be a fight to the death. Do not give your life for the daughter of Maeve.'

'I cannot turn back!' declared Ferdia. 'I have promised. Take the victory. It will be yours. I do not fear death. But if I went back now my honour would be broken in Rathcroghan. Maeve has been my undoing. Let us begin. What weapons should we use?'

That night they parted in silence and misery. Cuchulain slept with his charioteer on the north side of the river and Ferdia on the south.

When dawn came they put on full battle dress. Each felt this was the last day and they decided to use all their weapons.

They began quietly, but gradually the anger of warfare came upon them. They forgot their friendship and fought savagely as though they had been enemies all their lives.

The sparkling river was red with their blood and splashed over them as they struggled in the centre of the ford. Ferdia gave Cuchulain a blow with his gold-hilted sword that buried it in his body. Cuchulain leaped into the air but Ferdia caught him on his shield and flung him off. From each bank the charioteers shouted warnings and encouragement to their masters. But neither heard.

At last Curchulain called to Laeg for the Gae Bolg—the body spear—and Ferdia knew the fight was ending. He tried to protect himself with his great shield, but Cuchulain flung the terrible spear high and it pierced Ferdia's chest. He fell backwards and Cuchulain, running to him, lifted his friend and carried him to the north side.

'It is not right that I die by your hand, Hound of Ulster!' and Ferdia, and spoke no more.

Cuchulain fell fainting beside him. Laeg cried out, 'Rise up, Cuchulain! Maeve's army will be on us! There'll be no more single combats now!'

'Why should I rise again?' asked Cuchulain. 'I would sooner lie dead here than my friend Ferdia.'

But Laeg carried him away to Emer at Dun Dalgan. Maeve had the body of Ferdia placed in a grave with a mound over it and a pillar stone with his name and descent carved on it in Ogham.

9. The Rousing of Ulster

Still the warriors of Ulster lay helpless. Sualtam, Cuchulain's foster father, was no great fighter and dared not stand beside his son in the struggle against the Southern army. But when he saw Cuchulain was likely to be defeated, he mounted the Grey of Macha and rode through Ulster, trying to rouse the people.

'The Western raiders are upon us!' he shouted. 'Ulster is destroyed. Fight for your homes!'

But he could not stir them to battle.

He came to Emain Macha and there was Conor the King, Cathbad the Druid, chiefs and warriors, recovering from the Debility, yet still only half-awake. Sualtam rode the grey horse in among them.

'Cuchulain holds the Gap alone!' he cried. 'Arise and defend Ulster!'

They listened and nodded but could not move.

Angry and despairing, Sualtam tugged at the reins to turn the horse about. The grey reared, almost unseating him. Sualtam fell sideways upon the sharp rim of his shield, which severed his neck, and the head fell to the ground. Yet still it cried to the king, appealing to him not to abandon Cuchulain. Conor sleepily ordered a servant to place the head upon a pillar. Even then the voice sounded through the palace — 'Rise, King Conor, or your land will be taken from you! Awake, chieftains of Ulster! The invaders are upon us!'

The horse with its headless rider clattered out of the palace and still the head cried its warning.

Slowly the words sent their meaning into Conor's mind. The chieftains stared at one another in amazement and Macha's spell was lifted from them. Conor stood up and they stood with him. Quickly they seized their weapons while the king sent messengers throughout the land calling the men of Ulster together.

Maeve heard the Ultonians were advancing. Standing on the Hill of Slane she saw the Plain of Gorach covered with deer and other wild beasts.

'What brings them here?' she asked.

'They have been driven out of the forest by the Ulstermen,' replied Fergus Mac Roy, who watched beside her.

A mist rolled over the plain. From it came thunder and flashes of light.

RISE, KING CONOR, OR YOUR LAND WILL BE TAKEN FROM YOU!

'What is this?' asked Maeve.

'The mist is the deep breathing of the warriors as they march,' declared Fergus. 'The light is the flashing of their swords and spears and the thunder, the tumult of their chariots.'

'We have warriors to meet them!' said Maeve proudly.

'You will need them all!' Fergus Mac Roy told her.

Cuchulain heard the march of the Ultonians too and forgetting his grief over Ferdia's death, joined them in the battle at noon. Before dark the host of Connaught was in flight.

Cuchulain came up with Maeve as she reached the Shannon. She would not fly but halted her horses and waited.

'You are safe from me, Queen of Connaught, now that you are beaten,' he said.

Then, proud though she was, Maeve asked him to stop the slaughter of her retreating men.

'That will I gladly do,' replied Cuchulain.

And until the last of her men had crossed the river Cuchulain stood guard to see they went safely. Then he returned to Ulster and Maeve to Connaught.

The Brown Bull was before her and meeting the White Bull on the plain of Aei, the two great beasts charged one another. The Brown Bull caught Finnbenach on his horns and flung him to the ground, bellowing and trampling until the White Bull was dead. Then raging from Rathcroghan to Tara, the Donn of Cooley fell dead with exhaustion at the Ridge of the Bull.

After than peace was made between Maeve and Ulster.

10. The Vengeance of Maeve

In a little while Maeve forgot that but for Cuchulain her whole army would have been destroyed. She blamed him for her defeat in battle and for the death of the two bulls. She did not know which she regretted most—Finnbenach, who refused to stay in her herd, or Donn who had never been in it.

'There have never before been two such bulls in Ireland,' she said sorrowfully, 'nor ever will again.'

She thought and thought of her loss and her defeat until she determined on revenge.

Cuchulain lived happily with Emer. He had recovered from his wounds and slowly his strength came back. But still he grieved, for Ferdia's death was always at the back of his mind. He knew, too, that Maeve would never forgive him. She was too proud, too warlike, too much a lover of victory.

The wizard Catalin, who had been killed at the ford with his twenty-seven sons, left behind him his wife and six other children, three sons and three daughters. They were ugly, misshapen and loved evil. They were skilled in magic and Maeve gave them leave to do all the harm they could to Cuchulain.

While the Children of Catalin prepared charms and spells, Maeve sent secret messages to all the other enemies of the Hound of Ulster. Hearing that the Curse of Macha had fallen again upon the Ultonians she assembled her army and marched north.

Once again Cuchulain came to meet her. But the wizards made him think that wayside bushes and the trees of the forest were armed men. On every side he imagined in saw smoke rising from burning homes. He fought phantoms until his mind was filled with horror. Cathbad the Druid persuaded him to rest in a quiet glen where Niam, wife of his friend, Conall of the Victories, took care of him and made him promise not to leave the dun without her knowledge.

Bave, one of the daughters of Catalin, entered the dun in the form of a handmaiden, put a spell on Niam so that she wandered away and was lost in the woods. Bave then returned to the dun as Niam and bade Cuchulain go forth to save Ulster once more.

Cuchulain ordered Laeg to bring out his chariot and

harness the horses. The Grey of Macha resisted and when, at last, Laeg forced the yoke upon him, big tears poured down the Grey's face.

Cuchulain came to his own dun at Murthemney and Emer implored him not to be led by phantoms, but he would not listen and said goodbye. His mother, Dectera, was with Emer and she poured him a goblet of wine. As he put it to his lips the wine turned to blood and he flung it down.

'I shall not return from this battle,' he told them as he drove away.

He came to a ford. A girl was kneeling on the river bank, weeping as she washed a heap of bloodstained clothes. She lifted them from the water and Cuchulain saw they were his. But as he crossed the ford she vanished.

When Cuchulain came near Slieve Fuad, south of Armagh, his enemies had gathered to meet him and he drove straight at them. Hurling his spear, he sent it through nine men, killing them all. It was drawn out and flung back, missing Cuchulain, but striking Laeg, his friend and charioteer, who, calling 'Farewell, Hound of Ulster!' dropped on the floor of the chariot and died there.

Now the Grey of Macha was wounded and broke away, followed quickly by the Black. Cuchulain knew that he would never drive them again.

Maeve's warriors came near and Cuchulain looked calmly at them.

'My wounds have made me thirsty,' he said. 'Will you let me drink at the stream?'

They stood out of his way and, walking slowly, he went down to the river. He drank and washed away the blood, then came back to the bank.

A pillar stone stood there. He leaned against it and bound himself to it with his girdle. He took his sword in his right hand and laid his shield on the ground at his feet.

He died there, standing, with his face to his enemies, and the glory of Ulster died with him.

7

THE VOYAGE OF MAELDUN

NE morning in the graveyard at Doocloone, Maeldun, a young man who belonged to the Owens of Aran, was competing with a few friends in putting the stone. They were using the great blocks from the ruined church. The blocks were so heavy that Maeldun was winning easily for, though he was careless and easy-going, he was so strong that not one of his companions could beat him.

Among the crowd, who watched, was a young man who had fallen out of the game right at the start. He hated Maeldun, who was so good at running he could race a swift horse and was able to throw a ball so far there was little chance of finding it again.

He scowled angrily as Maeldun lifted a huge stone to his shoulder and flung it easily, laughing with pleasure at his own strength.

'Isn't it a pity you haven't something better to do than cast stones at Doocloone!' he jeered.

Maeldun turned to him in amazement.

'What could be better than casting stones on a clear, cold morning and the wind blowing from the sea?' he asked.

'If my father had been killed here and the church burned over him, I wouldn't be playing over his grave!' declared the other.

Maeldun no longer smiled. He walked over the rough and blackened ground until he stood in front of his enemy.

'You say my father was killed here!' he said.

'You seem to be the only one that doesn't know it,'

92

muttered the young man bitterly.

'Can you tell me who killed him?' asked Maeldun quietly.

The other drew back. He was sorry he had spoken. But Maeldun was gazing at him sternly, waiting.

'Raiders from Leix,' came the answer. 'They slew him on that spot where you were standing and burned the church over him.'

Maeldun went slowly away, very different from the gay young man who had set out that morning. He told his mother all he had heard.

'It is true!' she said sadly. 'I didn't tell you how Ailill, your father, died, for it spoiled my life and I didn't want it to spoil yours.'

'He must be avenged!' declared Maeldun. 'I'll seek out his murderers if I have to go to the end of the world to find them. How can I get to Leix?'

'Only by sea!'

Maeldun had no boat, so he decided to build a coracle. His two friends—German and Diurnan the Rhymer—went with him to the island Druid for advice.

The Druid listened to the story in silence.

'Sometimes forgiveness is better than vengeance,' he said. 'But if you must seek your father's enemy, make your coracle with three thicknesses of skin. Take only seventeen men with you. Begin building the boat on the first day of the new moon.

All the young men in the island who hoped to share in the expedition, offered to help. But Maeldun picked out the seventeen he wanted and would not allow any others to touch the boat.

At last it was launched, their stores taken on board and, as shouts of farewell came from their friends and families, they hoisted the sail.

As the wind caught it, Maeldun's three young foster brothers came running down the beach calling him to take them.

'Go home!' shouted Maeldun. 'You know I'm forbidden to take more than seventeen. Go home!.

93

But the boys jumped into the sea and swam after the boat. The waves were so rough they were being swept away when German pulled the smallest on board. Diurnan caught hold of another, while the third clambered in at the stern.

'It can make no difference,' muttered Maeldun. 'And I could not leave them to drown.'

When the wind dropped, the young men took turns at rowing. During the night, to give the rowers a rest, Maeldun once more put up the sail, though there was little wind. When morning came, they were near a small rocky island with a round fort standing in the middle. Spears came whizzing through the air from over the wall and a voice cried.

'I am the better man, for I killed Ailill of the Edge-of-Battle and burned the church of Doocloone over his body. Yet not one of his kinsmen has tried to find me and avenge his death. You have never done such a deed!'

'I never dreamt of finding my father's murderer in such a place!' exclaimed Maeldun.

'Our journey is over before we're properly started,' grumbled German, feeling quite disappointed.

'God has guided us!' said Diurnan the Rhymer.

Maeldun steered the boat in and, in spite of the shower of spears, which continued to fall about them, was about to leap on shore when a sudden squall swept them away from the island and all night long rain and wind beat on them until they had no notion where they could be.

'This is your fault!' exclaimed Maeldun to his foster brothers. 'You knew the druid had warned me, I must take only seventeen. This may be the beginning of our misfortunes!'

The boys looked so unhappy, Maeldun was ashamed of his anger.

'If they hadn't been so young, I might have chosen them myself,' he thought.

They drifted where wind and tide carried them, for Maeldun could not tell whether to go north or south, but hoped they might reach land where the inhabitants would direct them.

The third morning they heard the sound of waves beating against rocks and, as the sun rose, saw a flat, stony island. They were about to row in when a swarm of huge ants came scuttling along the beach. They looked so ferocious that Maeldun turned the boat round and they had to row their hardest, for the ants plunged into the sea and swam after them.

The voyagers came to many islands. There was one with built-up terraces and groves of trees with monstrous birds sitting in the branches. German and Diurnan landed on a flat island where they found an enormous race course. They heard shouts and saw gigantic white and brown horses running along the course, but they could see no people.

Diurnan the Rhymer sang of them—

> *Strange seas, strange islands*
> *Strange as dreams.*
> *I wonder if my eyes are closed.*
> *If still earth's sunlight gleams.*

Even Maeldun and his two friends were growing tired of the boat. They all longed for land where they could rest and stretch their limbs. The meat and meal they had brought with them was eaten and all they had was the fish they caught and rain water. When land, with trees growing to the edge of the shore, each loaded with golden apples, rose from the waves, they cheered with delight. As the boat drew nearer, they saw red swine running among the trees and kicking the trunks until the apples fell on the grass. Then they gorged themselves.

Maeldun and his companions gathered all the apples they had room for and, until they had eaten the last one, they needed no other food or drink.

But when the golden apples were finished, then indeed they knew hunger and thirst. The younger ones longed for home and doubted if they would ever see it again. Maeldun was listening to their complaints when he saw an island with a tall white tower rising from the centre. A great ram-

95

part was built about it and on each side were houses, white as if made of chalk.

Hiding the coracle behind some rocks, the men landed and went into the tower. They found a lofty hall with four low stone pillars in the middle and a great curving staircase at the end. There were no people, only a little black cat which was leaping from pillar to pillar. It looked at the Irish travellers but did not stop. On the walls hung rows of brooches, torcs of gold and silver, swords with gold and silver hilts and jewelled necklaces.

But what Maeldun liked better than all the treasures, was a table laid for a feast with roast meat and tall cups of wine.

'Was this left for us?' Maeldun asked the little cat.

It stopped to listen to him, then went on jumping. They sat down at the table and ate and drank until they were satisfied. Afterwards they lay on wide, cushioned seats which were all along one side of the hall, covered themselves with heavy silk quilts and slept as they had not slept since leaving Aran. Next day they took what was left of the food, but Maeldun wouldn't allow his companions to touch the brooches or swords, or the silken quilts and garments which lay on the seats.

As they were going out of the door, the youngest of Maeldun's foster brothers ran back and snatched an emerald necklace from its hook.

With a furious snarl, the black cat leaped at him and he fell in a heap of ashes on the floor.

Maeldun put the necklace back in its place, picked up the angry little creature and smoothed its fur. When they went out, the cat was once more jumping from pillar to pillar.

They began to lose count of time. Maeldun thought the young moon had appeared to them seven times. German was sure it must be twice as many. Diurnan couldn't remember at all.

They still had a little dry bread and, when that was eaten they kept the nets out the whole time.

Diurnan told stories and sang to keep his companions

"WAS THIS LEFT FOR US?"
MAELDUN ASKED THE LITTLE CAT

from thinking of their hardships.

'We should turn back,' said one. 'There were other houses on the island where the little black cat lived. This sea seems empty of fish, but we might find more food and drink. Isn't it foolish to wander all our lives! I could be happy there!'

'Do you remember what happened to my brother?' asked the second foster brother. 'I would not go back to that island for all the food in the world.'

While they talked the Rhymer was singing softly—

> *I longed to sail far where the sky*
> *Bends down and earth's great ocean ends.*
> *But now I long for little roads,*
> *For soft blue smoke, for home and friends.*

German and Maeldun watched. As the sun went down, a swift tide carried them into a harbour. Maeldun and the Rhymer climbed from the boat by narrow steps set in the harbour wall and saw before them a huge mill. A wide road led up to it and men hurried by, bent with the weight of heavy sacks.

There was no door but an open archway and the two strangers followed the men with the sacks into a vast chamber almost filled with a millstone.

In the dim light they saw a giant miller grinding away. The men emptied their sacks in a chamber at one side and filled them at the opposite end, where grey coarse flour fell in a heap.

The miller grinned at them. But there was no friendliness in his eyes.

'You have a right to see the work we do here,' he said. 'For half the corn of your country is ground in this mill. In those sacks is brought all that men grudge one another. You can carry away all you want. But take my advice and do not touch the corn we grind.'

'This is an evil task,' said Diurnan to Maeldun.

So they crossed themselves and went back to their comrades.

Once more they had nothing to eat but the fish which

came into their nets. They dried it in the sun. But only Maeldun, the Rhymer and German could eat it without grumbling. The men were sighing and groaning when they came to an island of black people, who wept and lamented all day, though there seemed no reason for their sorrow. Maeldun's second foster brother insisted on going ashore to learn what caused their misery. He, too, turned black and began weeping like the rest.

Maeldun sent two more to bring him back, but they also became black and began to weep. Four others went after them, but they wrapped their heads in their cloaks, so that they would not breathe the air of the island.

They managed to seize the two men but not the young foster brother and the boat had to sail without him. The two who were rescued couldn't explain what had happened to them. They saw others weeping so they wept. As the island faded into the distance, their own colour returned to them and they ceased weeping.

Many islands were scattered over that ocean and Diurnan declared that if they lived to be very old men, they would have tales to tell throughout the dark winter nights, yet need never tell the same story twice.

One island had a high fortress, frowning over the sea, with a bronze door in the centre. Leaving a guard on the ship, the others landed and came to a glass bridge, with bronze parapets crossing a wide moat which surrounded the fortress.

Keeping together, they stepped on the bridge but it flung them back. As they scrambled up, a woman came out of the fortress with a bucket in her hand. They shouted, but, without looking at them, she let down the bucket, drew water from the moat and returned to the fortress. Determined to enter, Maeldun struck the side of the bridge. The metal quivered and soft music came from it. His eyes closed. He slipped to the ground, asleep, and his companions lay sleeping beside him. The next day when they woke, the woman was coming out of the fortress with her bucket. She laughed at their foolishness, but they would not go away.

SHE CAME RIGHT ACROSS
THE BRIDGE AND THIS TIME
HER SMILE WAS FRIENDLY

Three days they tried to cross the bridge and each time they failed.

On the fourth day, when the woman came out on the bridge, she no longer carried a bucket, but was dressed in white silk with a golden circlet on her long fair hair and silver sandals on her feet.

She came right across the bridge and this time her smile was friendly.

'You are welcome, Maeldun, and you, Rhymer, and German, and every man of your crew. Come with me!'

They marched behind her over the glass bridge. The bronze gate of the fortress stood wide open and they went in with her. She put them at a table arranged with plates and goblets, but they were all empty. She filled them from her bucket, giving each man what he like best, of food and wine.

They lay on couches and their dreams were the happiest they had known. Yet when they woke they were crowded in their boat, the sail swelled in the wind and there was no trace on the sea of the island, the fortress, or the woman with the bucket.

'I never heard of these islands before,' said Diurnan the Rhymer. 'Strange that of all the ones that sailed from our country, none came this way.'

'Maybe they came, but could not return,' Maeldun told him. 'If we keep on, we shall come to the edge of the world.'

The wind had fallen and for days they took turns at the oars. Diurnan sang and recited poems which made them forget danger and loneliness, and kept their minds on the wonder of their wanderings.

He was silent when they saw a great square silver column rising up from the water. It towered into the sky so that they could not see the top. A silver net spread from it, so large they sailed through the mesh. Diurnan drew his sword and hacked off a piece.

'Do not destroy this work of mighty men!' Maeldun warned him.

'I want our tale to be believed when we return home,'

replied the Rhymer. 'If ever we reach Ireland again, I will lay this piece of silver on the High Altar of Armagh in honour of God's Name.'

A voice cried out from the top of the pillar—clear like a clarion. But they could not understand the words it spoke.

> *I saw a web float o'er the sea,*
> *A silver web dropped from the skies.*
> *I heard a voice that caught my soul,*
> *So loud, serene and wise. —*

murmured Diurnan to himself as they sailed on, marvelling.

A mist hid the silver column from them. But an island loomed up and, stepping from the boat, they waded to the beach, dragging the boat after them.

A wall rose before them. Walking round it to find an entrance, they came to a grassy mound and, climbing to the top, found themselves in sunshine. They sat there looking over the wall, which enclosed a mansion. At one side a marble bath sunk in the ground was being filled with water by seventeen girls. The clatter of a horse's hoofs sounded from the other side and a grandly dressed woman rode up to the house. She jumped down and a girl took the horse. Presently the rider went into the bath. A girl came through an unseen gateway in the wall and called to Maeldun and his men.

'The Queen invites you,' she said.

Gladly they obeyed, went down from the mound, in through the doorway they had not seen and up to the house. There a feast was ready. Mealdun sat opposite the Queen and each of his crew sat with one of the girls. At night they were given good beds and, when morning came, they were so refreshed all their troubles were forgotten.

But, when they prepared to go, the Queen stopped them.

'Stay here,' she said. 'You will never find your home again, so where is the sense in wandering from island to island, only to perish, miserably at the end? Stay here! You do not know the wonders of this island. There is no age or sickness here and there is room for all of you.'

Maeldun looked at his crew who had suffered so greatly. 'Shall we stay?' he asked.

'We will!' shouted each one of them.

The Queen told Maeldun that her husband had been King of the island and the seventeen girls were their daughters. Now the King was dead and she ruled. There were many other people on the island and all day she went among them, but came back at night.

Maeldun was happy there. So were they all for three months. But the crew soon forgot their hardships and began to long for their own country. It seemed to them that they had been away for years and they implored him to sail on.

'Where would we have a better life than we have here?' asked Maeldun. 'Let us stay a while.'

Even Diurnan and German were tired of the island and they told him that, if he wished to stay, they would go without him. But Maeldun could not bear to part with his friends and, to please him, they stayed though they grumbled all the time.

One day Diurnan and German decided to take the boat and depart at once. Maeldun declared he had changed his mind and would go with them.

The Queen was away trying to settle a quarrel among some of her people. They loaded the boat with provisions, put out the oars and pushed off. The Queen, riding home, saw their sail as it caught the wind. She had a ball of cord in her hand and, holding one end, flung the ball after them. Maeldun caught the ball and she drew them back.

Maeldun had been sorry to leave the island without saying goodbye, but now he was as determined as the others to depart. The next time the Queen was away from the fort, they boarded the boat again. They were scarcely an oar's length from the shore when she came riding up. Once more she flung the ball of string. Once more Maeldun caught it and they were drawn back.

Again this happened and the crew looked strangely at Maeldun.

'Why do you hold the ball?' asked German. 'If you

would sooner stay, why pretend? We can sail the boat without you!'

Indeed I don't hold it. The ball clings to my hand'' protested Maeldun. 'I am honest with you. I have been very happy here, but I long for home.'

So the next time, one of the crew caught the ball and when he could not let go, Diurnan cut off his hand and it fell into the sea. Away sped the boat. But the Queen on her horse wept, so that tears poured down her face and the seventeen girls wept with her, while from all over the island rose cries of sorrow.

Maeldun, with tears in his eyes, looked backward, as long as he could see the island where he had been treated as a king.

There was no wind and the soft air made them lazy so that the oars barely feathered the heaving sea. Yet the boat moved swiftly in a current which carried them round an island thickly wooded on one half and with a wide stretch of grassland covering the other. Sheep grazed beside a lake and when the current brought them in to a curved bay, they found an ancient fort and a small church where an old monk was saying Mass.

'Who are you, holy man?' asked Maeldun, when they came out into the sunshine once more.

'I am one of the monks who went on an ocean pilgrimage with St Brendan of Birr,' said the monk. 'And I am the only one left alive.'

The old man had so much to tell them and was so pleased with their company that they stayed with him while they cleaned the boat, mended the sail and collected food.

One day Maeldun saw a dark cloud, driving from the south-west. It came so quickly he guessed it could not be a real cloud and as it drew near, he saw that it was a great eagle with faltering wings, carrying a red-berried branch in its talons. It dropped beside the lake and began eating the berries, big as grapes. Some of the juice and skins fell into the lake until the water looked like wine.

Diurnan and German coming in search of Maeldun, hid

ONCE MORE SHE FLUNG THE BALL OF STRING

with him among the trees and watched the great bird, fearing if they showed themselves, it would seize them in its curved claws and carry them off, though it seemed old and sick, and its dull plumage was thin. But when Maeldun walked down to the lake, the bird took no notice and presently the others followed him. They gathered some of the fallen berries and still the eagle did not look at them.

As they walked away, two smaller eagles flew down and began cleaning and smoothing the old bird's feathers. The next day the birds were still there, and the day after the big eagle plunged into the lake. When it came out the watchers saw that its plumage was clean and glossy, old age had gone from it and it was a young, strong eagle who flew away out of sight, its helpers trying to keep up with it.

'Let us become young like the eagle,' suggested Diurnan. 'I am old from hardship and travelling.'

'No! No!' cried Maeldun. 'The bird may have poisoned the water.'

But Diurnan slipped in, swam in the lake and drank the crimson water. From that day he was never tired or sick. His eyes were always clear and keen, his teeth strong and, to the last hour of his long life, he was like a young man.

They said goodbye to the old monk of Birr and sailed on.

Diurnan was singing about the eagle when they heard loud laughter and shouts of enjoyment. Towards dawn they reached an island where they could see men and women dancing, tossing balls to one another and laughing all the time.

'There's no sense in landing here,' said Maeldun.

But as several men longed to know what made the islanders so merry he let them draw lots for the one who should go on shore. His own foster brother, the last of the three, was winner. The moment he set foot on the island, he began to laugh and jig about like the others. Maeldun shouted to him to come back, but he would not and, in the end, they left him there, still laughing and dancing.

Maeldun's three brothers were gone from the ship, one dead, one on the island of the black mourners and now, the

106

last of them left behind with the laughing people.

'Maybe our voyage is coming to an end,' said Maeldun. 'I am tired of strange places, yet how can I return without avenging my father!'

Just then they saw a white patch floating on the water.

They thought it a wounded seabird, but when they came up with it, they found an old, old man, covered in his long white hair and beard which grew to his feet. He lay on a broad flat rock without shelter.

'Come with us in the boat!' urged Maeldun, who was sorry for the man's desolation. 'How have you come to such misery?'

'Do not grieve for me,' the old man told them. 'Listen, now! I belonged to Tory Island. I was born and grew up there. Have you heard of the monastery of Tory? I was the cook. All around me were good, holy men. Yet daily I took the food and sold it to passing ships for grand clothes and golden ornaments and even manuscripts bound in jewelled leather. Because I wasn't found out I grew proud and thought myself the cleverest man on Tory.

'One day I filled a boat with all my treasures and started away so that I could live grandly where no one knew I had been a cook. A storm came up and I was terrified. But, when the wind dropped, the boat lay becalmed and there before me was an angel standing on the water.

'Where are you going?' he asked.

'To lead a comfortable, pleasant life for the rest of my days,' I told him.

'You would not think it pleasant if you could see the demons gathered round you. Because of your greed and pride, the boat will not move and unless you do as I tell you, your road will take you straight to hell.'

I was frightened and began to feel sorry as well.

'Tell me what to do?' I said.

'Throw all you have stolen into the sea,' commanded the angel. 'And where the boat brings you, there you must stay.

'I threw out my beautiful clothes, the jewelled books and gleaming ornaments, until all I had left was a little wooden cup which really was my own. The boat brought me to this bare rock and here I have been for seven years. Otters bring me salmon from the sea and every day this cup is filled with good wine. I have all eternity to think about and I never feel cold or wet.'

Then Maeldun told his story.

'You will find the man who killed your father, Maeldun,' said the cook. 'But don't kill him. What good would it do your father? God has saved you from great dangers. And have you never done wrong? Forgive your enemy, then you will go back to your own country in peace.'

Maeldun thanked him and they went on.

As darkness came they reached a small island.

'We have seen this before,' said Maeldun.

It was the island where the murderer of his father lived.

The coracle grated gently on the strand. They lifted it up and went quietly to the fort. The gate was open. The door of the hall where the company sat at their evening meal was open and there were no men on guard.

'What would you do if you saw Maeldun?' asked one.

'I would give him a great welcome!' declared the chief man, the slayer of Ailell. 'For if he lives he has had great toil and suffering through my evil doing, and I would ask him to forgive me.'

Maeldun beat on the door with his spear.

'Who is there?' cried the chief.

'Maeldun is here!' he answered.

They entered in peace and were given such a welcome it made the whole voyage seem worthwhile. Diurnan the Rhymer told the story of the wanderings. The night went on and another day had come before that story was ended.

They went home easily and in comfort. But the Rhymer journeyed on to Armagh and laid upon the High Altar the piece of wrought silver he had hewn from the silver net.

There he again told the story of the Voyage of Maeldun.

ENCHANTED IRISH TALES
Patricia Lynch

Enchanted Irish Tales tells of ancient heroes and heroines, fantastic deeds of bravery, magical kingdoms, weird and wonderful animals ... This new illustrated edition of classical folktales, retold by Patricia Lynch with all the imagination and warmth for which she is renowned, rekindles the age-old legends of Ireland, as exciting today as they were when first told. This collection includes:

Conary Mór and the Three Red Riders
The Long Life of Tuan Mac Carrell
Finn Mac Cool and the Fianna
Oisin and the Land of Youth
The Kingdom of the Dwarfs
The Dragon Ring of Connla
Mac Datho's Boar
Ethne

THE CHILDREN'S BOOK OF
IRISH FOLKTALES
Kevin Danaher

These tales are filled with the mystery and adventure of a land of lonely country roads and isolated farms, humble cottages and lordly castles, rolling fields and tractless bogs. They tell of giants and ghosts, of queer happenings and wondrous deeds, of fairies and witches and of fools and kings.

IRISH LEGENDS FOR THE VERY YOUNG
NIAMH SHARKY

Aimed at early readers and written to be read aloud to young children of five to eight, *Irish Legends for the Very Young* contains a new retelling of three of the classic, best loved Irish legends: 'The Children of Lir', 'How Setanta Became Cúchulainn' and 'Oisín in Tír na nÓg'. Retold with the viewpoint of the young reader in mind, these tales are charmingly illustrated by the author.

IRISH FAIRY STORIES FOR CHILDREN
EDMUND LEAMY

In these stories we read all about the exciting adventures of Irish children in fairyland. We meet the fairy minstrel, giants, leprechauns, fairy queens and wonderful talking animals in Tir na nÓg.

THE IRISH LEPRECHAUN BOOK
SELECTED BY MARY FEEHAN

Leprechauns are supposed to know where pots of gold are buried and they guard this secret very well. They are very hard to ensnare, and if you manage to catch one then you must hold him firmly and never, even for a second, take your eyes off him because in the blink of an eye he will disappear and he will use every trick he knows to escape – so be warned.

GOLDEN APPLES
IRISH POEMS FOR CHILDREN

Edited by JO O'DONOGHUE

Here is a magical new collection of Irish poems for children featuring cats, dogs, squirrels, sheep and lambs – and of course leprechauns and fairies. There are stirring ballads and interesting grown-ups like My Aunt Jane and the Dublin Piper. Great poets like Yeats, Kavanagh, MacNeice and Heaney are included, but also the anonymous versifiers who gave us such gems as 'Brian O'Linn' and 'I'll Tell My Ma'.

Golden Apples is a collection to treasure.

STRANGE IRISH TALES FOR CHILDREN

EDMUND LENIHAN

Strange Irish Tales for Children is a collection of four exciting stories, by seanchaí Edmund Lenihan, which will entertain and amuse children of all ages. The stories tell of the hair-raising adventures of the Fianna and about Fionn MacCumhail's journey to Norway in search of a blackbird. There is a fascinating tale about 'The Strange Case of Seán na Súl' whose job was to kidnap people to take them away to a magic island. 'Taoscán MacLiath and the Magic Bees' is a story about the exploits of this very famous druid and about how he packed his spell-books and took himself off to the conference held by the druids of the Seven Lands.

IRISH MYTHS AND LEGENDS

EOIN NEESON

Eoin Neeson delves deep into the past and comes up with plenty of intrigue, romance and excitement in these fascinating stories about our Firbolg and Milesian forbears. He retells his stories with a directness and simplicity which make them refreshingly modern. *Irish Myths and Legends* contains stories of 'The Tale of the Children of Tuireann', 'The Wooing of Etain', 'The Combat at the Ford', and 'Deirdre and the Sons of Usna'.

A HISTORY OF IRISH FAIRIES

CAROLYN WHITE

Whether you believe in fairies or not, you cannot ignore them, and here for the first time is *A History of Irish Fairies*. Having no stories directly from the fairies themselves, we must rely on descriptions by mortal men and women. A large part of the book is concerned with the relations between mortals and fairies, so that the reader may determine the best way to behave whenever he encounters fairies. You can read about the Far Darrig, Merrows and Silkies, Banshees and Keening, the Lianhan Shee, Pookas, Dullahans and Ghosts.